HIS TO PROTECT

AVA GRAY

ALSO BY AVA GRAY

CONTEMPORARY ROMANCE

Mafia Kingpins Series

His to Own

His to Protect

Harem Hearts Series

3 SEAL Daddies for Christmas

Small Town Sparks

Her Protector Daddies

The Billionaire Mafia Series

Knocked Up by the Mafia

Stolen by the Mafia

Claimed by the Mafia

Arranged by the Mafia

Charmed by the Mafia

Alpha Billionaire Series

Secret Baby with Brother's Best Friend

Just Pretending

Loving The One I Should Hate

Billionaire and the Barista

Coming Home

Doctor Daddy

Baby Surprise

A Fake Fiancée for Christmas

Hot Mess

Love to Hate You - The Beckett Billionaires

Just Another Chance - The Beckett Billionaires

Valentine's Day Proposal

The Wrong Choice - Difficult Choices

The Right Choice - Difficult Choices

SEALed by a Kiss

The Boss's Unexpected Surprise

Twins for the Playboy

When We Meet Again

The Rules We Break

Secret Baby with my Boss's Brother

Frosty Beginnings

Silver Fox Billionaire

Taken by the Major

Daddy's Unexpected Gift

Playing with Trouble Series:

Chasing What's Mine

Claiming What's Mine

Protecting What's Mine

Saving What's Mine

The Beckett Billionaires Series:

Love to Hate You

Just Another Chance

Standalone's:

Ruthless Love

The Best Friend Affair

PARANORMAL ROMANCE

. . .

Maple Lake Shifters Series:

Omega Vanished

Omega Exiled

Omega Coveted

Omega Bonded

Everton Falls Mated Love Series:

The Alpha's Mate

The Wolf's Wild Mate

Saving His Mate

Fighting For His Mate

Dragons of Las Vegas Series:

Thin Ice

Silver Lining

A Spark in the Dark

Fire & Ice

Dragons of Las Vegas Boxed Set (The Complete Series)

Standalone's:

Fiery Kiss

Wild Fate

BLURB

He's not going to take no for an answer, and he's willing to pay his way in...

VIN

Nothing burns like love. And I've been through the flames once already, so that's been there, done that situation.

Not looking to fall in love means I want one thing only - a gorgeous woman in my arms, and an empty bed by sunrise.

Until I meet Hannah Everson at a virginity auction, and buy her to be my wife.

Because that's how this ends. Gorgeous, innocent Hannah never stood a chance against a kingpin like me.

HANNAH

Want to know one thing that's guaranteed to ruin your life for good?

Borrowing money from the wrong people, then owing them something you don't have.

Sure, the money paid for my mom's medical bills, but she's gone now… and I have a debt to pay.

When I'm forced to sell the only valuable thing left about me, I end up in the lair of a mafia prince.

He says he'll protect me, but is Vincentius Rossi someone I can trust?

Or will his overpowering love break us?

His to Protect **is book two of the Mafia Kingpins series. This is a full-length standalone novel with these tropes: age gap, forced proximity, surprise pregnancy. Expect a happily ever after ending!**

1

HANNAH

*I*t's official. *I hate my life.*

Normally, I'm a pretty positive and happy person, but these last six months have been absolute hell. I feel like I've been dragged through the wringer then chewed up and spit out. Multiple, soul-crushing times.

With a weary sigh, I punch out on the clock in the diner's back room, untie my apron and stuff it into my bag. I've been on my feet for the past eight hours and they're aching because I've been running around like a mad woman, trying to serve customers and deal with being short-staffed all day. I can't wait to get home and soak them. When the diner gets busy, it's good because the time goes by fast, but it's also bad because now I'm exhausted. Like bone-deep weary and I feel like I could sleep for an entire week. No, scratch that. I could sleep for a month. I'd planned to go through my mom's things, but I don't have the energy for it. Mentally or physically.

Last week, I lost my mom, my closest confidante and very best friend, to cancer. It's the worst-damn disease and watching someone you love slowly lose her battle and waste away to nothing—into someone you barely recognize—is the most awful thing in the world. I wouldn't wish the painful experience on my worst enemy.

God, I could use a break. Shoving my ponytail off my shoulder, I duck out the back door and it occurs to me that no matter how hard I work or how many extra hours I pick up, I won't be able to pay back the money I borrowed any time soon. Hell, any time this century.

However, when your mother has cancer, but not insurance, a daughter does what she has to do. After hearing about my money problems, a friend at the diner, Ray the cook, connected me with a shady guy he knows who hooked me up with a loan. I didn't think twice, just signed the dotted line on some papers, cashed the check and made sure my mom got the best care available. Treatment is insanely expensive and she battled hard for the better part of last year. Last week, hospice stepped in, provided the necessary painkillers and everything else she needed. After crying my eyes out, knowing there was nothing else I could do, I forced myself to say goodbye as she died.

Shit. The salty sting of tears threaten once again and I try to swallow them down. It's impossible, though. I've been grieving since way before she died. Technically, since the terminal diagnosis. Of all the people to get lung cancer, why her? She never smoked a cigarette in her life. The sick irony of it all hits me like a sucker punch. Chemo and radiation only did so much for her. The cancer metastasized fast —from her lungs to her liver and finally, to her brain.

Swiping a tear off my cheek, I hustle across the street before the light changes to "do not walk." Luckily, my apartment is only three blocks away, but my feet are screaming with every single step.

Almost there, I tell myself. *Then you can soak your tootsies in a nice warm tub of sudsy bathwater.* After that I'll fall into my bed and temporarily forget all about my life and the humongous debt hanging over my head, weighing me down. It's truly suffocating, but I had no idea who the loan shark was or the kind of man I was dealing with, only that I needed money fast. But Ray told me a few stories, after I borrowed the money, of course, about what happened to people who didn't pay Dexter Creed back. No one has come looking for payment yet, but I'm so edgy and it feels like I'm living on borrowed time. And that's a damn scary place to be.

Paranoia sets in and I force myself to speed-walk once I reach my block. The sooner I get safely in my apartment and lock the door, the better I'll feel. All sorts of thoughts fill my head about movies where the person doesn't pay back a loan shark on time. Mafia stuff where they send enforcers to warn them and they break their arms and legs. Or, they seal their feet in a block of cement and toss them off a boat so they can sleep with the fish. Hugging my arms across my chest, a shiver runs through me. And it isn't because of the slight chill in the late spring air.

Normally, I love May. Everything is suddenly and completely alive again. The plants are green and the flowers are in full bloom. April's rain showers have gone away and they leave so much beauty in their wake. It's still not hot yet and I can open the windows and get a nice, refreshing breeze. I live in Brooklyn, so it's not nearly as expensive or crowded as Manhattan, but it's definitely come a long way from where it used to be.

However, I'm not feeling the beautiful May vibes right now. Instead, I keep looking over my shoulder because I have the strangest sensation that someone is following me. Yet, every time I'm brave enough to look back, there's no one there. Just me and my overactive imagination. Which, I suppose, is a good thing.

I know someone will be coming, though. Very soon. My best bet is they give me more time and they let me work out a payment plan. I don't see why that would be a problem, especially after I explain what happened with my mom and why I needed the money in the first place. It's not like I blew it all on a shopping spree or bought extravagant items like a car or house. No, nothing selfish like that. I paid for my mom to be comfortable in her final days. Anyone with half a heart would cut me some slack and allow me some extra time to pay the debt off. Wouldn't they?

Although after everything I've heard about Dexter Creed, I question if he has an actual heart.

As much as I'm hoping my lender will be sympathetic, I seriously doubt Creed cares a whit about my circumstances. Why would he? I've never met him personally, but I have heard plenty of rumors and hearsay—that he's a cold, calculating businessman who doesn't forgive or forget. And, still knowing this, I took money from him, anyway.

God. What was I thinking?

I wasn't thinking. I was too lost in taking care of my mother and over-whelmed by sorrow because I knew I was going to lose her sooner rather than later.

And now here we are. She's gone, but never forgotten. The money I borrowed—all fifty thousand dollars—is also gone. I used it to pay the hospital and the specialists for medicine and treatments. Then I used what little I had left to bury her. And, sadly, that wasn't even enough.

Squeezing my eyes shut, I pretend my life didn't change so drasti-cally in the last six months. If I hope and wish hard enough, maybe I can open my apartment door and see my mom inside. Somehow step back in time. She'd smile, ask me how my day was and tell me she'd baked cookies and that dinner would probably be almost ready.

Not anymore, though. Now, it's just me. My dad took off when I was still a baby, so it's always been just me and my mom. I think this is why her death has hit me extra hard. She was truly my best friend and, without her, my life is never going to be the same.

When I reach the old brick building where I live, I pause and dig down in my bag, searching for my keys. Returning to a dark and empty apartment sucks. It's a little depressing to be all by myself, but what can I do? I'm not in the right place to try dating, so maybe I'll get a cat. Not like I have a lot of options.

Snagging my keys off the bottom of my cluttered bag, I stick them in the lock and twist. The old door creaks open and I step inside. The building is old, but fairly well maintained. Well, kind of, anyway. Sure, it could use a fresh coat of paint and when it rains, it smells a little musty, but I've always felt safe and I'm appreciative of the nice neighbors. When my mom was sick, a couple of the women on my floor brought me dinner a few times. It was a kind gesture. Trust me, the last thing on my mind had been cooking, so their thoughtfulness touched me. It had been nice and not many people go out of their way to be nice anymore.

Granted, Liza Dixon is a bit on the nosy side, but she's older and lives by herself. Without much going on in her own life other than her soap operas, game shows and two cats, I think she lives vicariously through the rest of us. She always knows what's going on with everyone in the building and is a bit of a gossip.

Oh, God. I'm going to turn into Eliza Dixon. The thought hits me hard as I stop to open my mailbox. I'm going to be a lonely, old cat lady with no family, no prospects, no future. One day I'll die and no one will even know. I suppose someone will stumble upon my corpse eventually but, by then, the cat may have already eaten my face off.

Ugh. That settles it, I decide, reaching into the narrow slot for my mail. *No cat.*

Shoving what mostly looks like ads and bills into my bag, I shut the mailbox and head toward the stairs. I'm on the second floor and tend to avoid taking the rickety elevator whenever possible. It's shaky, breaks down more often than it runs, and I always have an overwhelming sense of doom every single time I step into that dimly-lit cab. I always get the overwhelming and awful feeling that the cables are going to snap or something and I'm going to plummet to my death. Although, I guess it's safe to say I'd probably survive a drop from the second floor to the first. However, the way my luck has been going recently, I don't want to chance it or tempt fate.

No, thank you. It'll be the stairs for me.

Swinging my bag over my shoulder, I hike up the slightly uneven wooden stairs, trying to ignore my aching feet. No matter how comfortable my shoes were when I first put them on, nothing is comfy after running around in them for over eight hours. The stairwell seems to go up and up with no end in sight. When I finally reach the top, I let out a little sigh. Almost there. There's not much in my fridge and I'm contemplating heading straight into a bath followed by bed. I've lost weight because of the extra stress and anxiety, but I don't let myself splurge on food or going out to dinner. Ever. It's just a luxury I can't quite afford right now and that's okay. I suppose I could eat that packet of Ramen noodles in my cupboard after I soak my poor tired feet.

I'm almost halfway down the hall when I abruptly stop short. My eyes land on my apartment door and it's slightly ajar. Not all the way open, but just enough that I notice. Did someone break in? There's no way I forgot to lock it. Although I've never had a problem, my neighborhood could definitely be better.

God. Just when my life can't get any worse, it takes a plunge. Fate must really hate me.

Standing there, I chew on my lower lip and wonder what to do. Should I go inside and check things out? What if someone is still in there, though? Doubtful, but who knows? But, who's going to break in and hang around? Unless they just got inside. My leery mind is spinning with possibilities.

I suppose I could always go to my neighbor's place and call the police from there. That seems like the smartest thing to do. Besides, maybe Eliza saw or heard something. She's such a busy body that I wouldn't be surprised. She might even have something useful to tell me and the cops.

I'm turning toward her place when the door to my apartment suddenly opens all the way and a man steps out. My heart and feet freeze at the same time and I swallow hard. He's big and burly with a mean look in his beady eyes. I'm holding my breath, not sure what the hell to do when he gives me an oily smile.

"Are you Hannah Everson?"

He possesses a gravelly voice that sends a shiver down my spine and I automatically take a step back.

"No." The lie slips from my lips. *C'mon, Eliza. This would be the perfect time to open your door and put that busy body of yours into action.*

But, of course, her door remains firmly shut and it's so quiet up here that I wonder if anyone is even home. There are four apartments total on my floor and I'm not hearing a sound from within any of them. *Figures.* Normally, I hear Eliza's TV playing at top volume and the kids next door to me are screaming and the couple across the way are fighting with each other.

Right now, though? Not a peep. Crickets. You'd think I was in a cloistered monastery somewhere surrounded by nuns who took a vow of silence.

God help me, I think. Can I please just get a break?

The giant takes a threatening step closer. "You sure about that? Because you look an awful lot like her."

He doesn't believe me. I can see it in his dark eyes and panic consumes me when he starts stalking toward me. Too scared to think logically, I spin around and do the only thing I can do—I turn and bolt.

My achy feet are long forgotten as I race back to the stairs, fly down them and shove my way out the front door and back outside. I just need to find a group of people, some life, a crowd, anything.

Anything to deter the man who is now chasing me.

"Hannah!" he yells, stomping after me. "You owe my boss some money."

My entire body breaks out in a clammy sweat when he growls those ominous words and I don't bother turning around. Dexter Creed wants his money and I don't have it. I knew this day was coming, but now what? I can't spend the rest of my life running and hiding.

Shit. Maybe I don't have a choice. All I know is I am absolutely terrified and I need to get as far away from Creed's enforcer as possible. Because one thing is clear. That huge behemoth chasing me? He wouldn't just break an arm or a leg.

He'd kill me.

I could see the violent storm brewing in his black eyes. I'm not stupid enough to stop and chat with him, either. All he wants is Creed's money and when he finds out I'm broke, that I don't even have twenty dollars in my bank account, he's going to end me.

And, as much as I miss my mom, I'm not exactly ready to see her again just yet on the other side. Pushing myself harder, I spot a couple of kids hanging on the corner outside the small convenience store up ahead. A sliver of hope fills me. Maybe, just maybe, I can find someone to help me.

I sure hope so. If not, I'm in big trouble.

God, I hate my life. But that doesn't mean I'm going down without a fight. My mom raised me tougher than that.

2

VIN

I listen closely to the proposal my older brother Miceli is offering me and it occurs to me that this might be the very distraction I need. He wants me to take over running the wine business branch we have here in the States. Of course, the original Rossi Vineyard and estate is located in southern Sicily and our parents still live there. The soil is extremely fertile and my dad oversees the growing of Nero d'Avola, the most important red wine grape in Sicily. Our wines are of the highest quality and in high demand all over the world. Taking on the role of President of Rossi Vineyard is huge and would keep me busy. Too busy to dwell on why I haven't been happy lately. Hell, lately? Who am I kidding? I haven't been truly happy in years.

Because something is missing. I can't explain what or why I've been feeling this way, but there's a hole and, no matter what I do, I can't seem to fill it. Maybe being sucked into the winery business will help by giving me something to focus on. Hopefully, this restless, empty ache will finally go away.

While Miceli starts talking about the company's most-recent profit report, I nod and pretend I'm all ears. But, really, my mind starts drifting. Truth be told, I was never a numbers man. That's Enzo, all the way. My younger brother could explain profit margins, losses, gains and everything in between without blinking an eye or pausing to take a breath—absolutely anything that has to do with the stock market is in his blood. Plus, he's a genius at picking stocks. We all have portfolios with him and he makes me more money in one year than some people make after working ten years. And I don't have to lift a finger.

So, do I technically need to head up a company and add all that stress on my plate? No. Enzo makes this family money in his sleep and we have enough to last several lifetimes. But I need something to help fix this strange and overwhelming feeling inside me. This need for... *something*.

It's almost like something is missing. Even though I don't know what exactly, I can be certain it isn't a serious relationship. I do *not* need a woman in my life. That much is for absolute certainty. Okay, so let me rephrase that. Maybe my body would like a warm, welcoming female companion to satisfy the urges of my very lonely dick. Because there's no denying it—I'm a thirty-two year old man with sexual needs and wants. But, what I don't want is to be burned again. I still have the scars and I'm not naive enough to go down that path again.

Love is a fool's paradise. The simple truth is that instant attraction is nothing more than lust. Pure unadulterated sexual desire. A body's immediate reaction to simply want to mate with another body. Those stupid chemicals released in the brain help trick a person into thinking he or she is "in love." But, the truth is, the yearning is merely a desire for physical release. Nothing more.

I learned that the hard way. It was a damn painful lesson that took me a long time to come to terms with and process. But now I know that love isn't for me. It's just...too damn painful.

Pulling in a deep breath, I nod and pretend interest in the slides my brother is flipping through on the white screen with a little clicker. Miceli is always so organized, determined and he's the sharpest leader I've ever encountered when it comes to ruling an empire. He's not only book smart, but also street smart. And he's ruthless in both arenas. If someone crosses him, or anyone in our family, Miceli will end them. Not long ago, Rocco Bianche, a rival, kidnapped Miceli's wife, Alessia. Big mistake. We managed to rescue her and it all ended on a happy note. Well, except for Bianche. He's no longer breathing.

That's what happens when you cross the Rossi family.

"Earth to Vin."

I look up, caught daydreaming, and give Miceli a lopsided grin. "I'm listening."

"Really?" Miceli rolls his eyes. "Then what did I just say?"

"You said it's time to wrap this meeting up, big brother."

"No, I didn't," he states dryly. "But nice try."

Beside me, Angelo chuckles and I know my youngest brother is ready to get the hell out of here even more than I am. Ang has the attention span of a gnat and would much rather be out traveling the world or trying to seduce some poor, unsuspecting woman. He's a consummate player and, I swear, he has a new girlfriend every week. Probably because he gets bored easily and no one has managed to keep his interest for longer than a few weeks. Glancing over at him, I can't help but be a little envious. He's so damn carefree, lives his life to the fullest and nothing ever seems to bother him.

Me, on the other hand? I'm the broody, moody, sensitive one who got his damn heart broken because he was stupid enough to give it to the wrong woman. And, five years later, I still can't get over it. No matter how hard I try. Even in my own head, it sounds pathetic.

I truly thought I was going to spend the rest of my life with Cynda and then I caught her fucking another man. Bitch. My heart shattered on the spot and I vowed to never let a woman that close to me again.

Since my ill-fated love affair with Cynda, I've come up with a series of rules for myself which will prevent anything similar from ever happening again. Celibacy isn't an option, so now I'm careful to keep my walls high and my heart guarded. Locked down completely. Fucking is fine; falling in love is not. As soon as the fucking is over, I leave. There's no cuddling or whispered words, no sweet lies exchanged. And I don't ever bring a woman back home to my place or allow her in my bed. Instead, I always get a hotel room or we go back to her place. The less personal it is, the better.

With all my rules, it's actually been a while since I've had a night of letting loose and enjoying a woman for an hour or so. I never linger and I make that clear upfront because I don't play games or want to lead anyone on. I'm not a liar like Cynda and I make my true intentions clear immediately—I'm not looking for anything serious. Not now, not tomorrow, not ever. All I can offer is some late-night debauchery. Then, I'm gone.

Oh, and I never do repeats. I'm a one and done man. It's just easier that way and prevents any kind of emotional entanglement for either of us.

"So, what's the verdict?" Enzo asks, crossing his arms over his broad chest. "Are you stepping up, Vin?"

I nod. "Yeah, why the hell not? I really enjoy dealing with the Rossi Vineyard side of things. Thanks, Miceli, for believing in me."

"We all believe in you, bro." Miceli slaps a hand between my shoulder blades. "You're going to have to go into the office every day, though. You realize that, right?"

My mouth edges up, along with my middle finger. "Kinda figured," I say dryly.

Angelo visibly shivers. Sometimes, I think my youngest brother is allergic to offices. "Look on the bright side, Vin. Now, you can hire yourself a hot-ass assistant."

"You are going to need an executive assistant," Enzo states.

"My advice?" Miceli shoots me a serious look. "Choose a man or a married woman over sixty."

I roll my eyes. "I don't sleep with employees."

"There's always the temptation," Enzo comments and we all look at him. He practically lives at his office downtown. "Why're you all looking at me like that? I'd never eat where I shit. I'm just saying it's been known to happen—with other people."

"Yeah, let's all just keep it that way." Miceli drops the clicker on the table.

"Guess we can't all be as lucky as you, Miceli," Angelo says teasingly. "A gorgeous wife and adorable son—#goals."

"Ang, you wouldn't know what to do if you were stuck with the same woman day in and day out."

In perfect Angelo fashion, he starts scratching his neck like a rash just cropped up and shifts in his seat, looking extremely uncomfortable at the thought. "To each his own, right? I can't help it. When I, ah, shop, I prefer to buy the variety pack. Having the same meal day in and day out gets a little…boring. No offense, Miceli."

But my older brother just grins, hearts and flowers in his eyes. "None taken. You poor foolish boys have no idea. Meeting and marrying Alessia was the best thing that ever happened to me. She's my reason for everything."

Enzo shakes his head. "I still can't believe the Great and Powerful Miceli Rossi has been brought down to his knees by a tiny, wisp of a woman."

"Alessia may be small, but she's mighty."

"We're happy for you, though, bro." Enzo pushes up out of his seat and glances down at the ridiculously expensive watch on his wrist. "I gotta get back to the office and make this family some more money. Alessia is perfect for you and baby Nico is going to call me his favorite uncle after I show him how to make millions of dollars in only a day."

"You wish!" Angelo pops up. "I'm going to take that kid all over the world and show him how to have fun. How to enjoy life and meet beautiful women."

Miceli frowns and places a hand over his chest. "Nico is two months old. I don't want to think about him talking yet, much less globetrotting with his playboy uncle. It's enough to give me heart palpitations."

My brothers and I laugh. At thirty-five, Miceli is still in excellent shape, but I have noticed the slight silver coming in at his temples. Hell, I plucked a gray hair two days ago and I'm three years younger. I wish we would stop aging and just stay how we are, but I know that's impossible. Life doesn't stop for anyone no matter how powerful you are or how much money is in your bank account.

"Alright, see you guys later. I have a hot date. I'm thinking of picking her up in my helicopter. I don't know, though. Too much?"

I can't help but laugh.

"Maybe a little over the top for a first date," Miceli comments dryly.

"Oh, I don't know," Enzo says, a twinkle in his dark eyes. "I say do it. Show off your piloting skills. You can use all the extra help you can get."

"Yeah, right," Angelo says, blowing that last comment off. "Your boy does not need any extra help when it comes to getting a woman. Not even an ounce." With a salute and a smirk, Angelo jogs out.

Damn, I wish I could be more like him sometimes, I think, and roll my eyes. Not a care in the world.

"Vin, we'll have you start at the office on Monday," Miceli tells me. "Enjoy the rest of your week."

"Gee, thanks. You know it's Friday already, right?"

"Work doesn't stop on the weekend." Miceli grins and I let out a sigh, hoping this new position doesn't send me into an early grave. Or, give me an entire head of gray hair. "I'll see you guys later."

"Great," I murmur and head toward the door, along with Enzo. We walk out of Miceli's corner office and pass down a hallway, through the foyer and out a set of glass doors.

"So, what're you up to tonight? Any plans?"

I look over at my polished brother, dressed in some high-end suit, and shake my head. "Nah. I was thinking of ordering in and maybe finishing that new show I started binging. It's pretty good about the former Navy SEAL guy out for revenge. Have you seen it?"

"You're kidding, right? I might have every streaming channel available and watch my TV monitors all the time, but the only thing I view are stocks."

Damn, maybe I'm not the only one around here who needs to get out more. The thought hits me hard and I run a hand through my hair. "Do you ever feel like life is passing you by? Or, that maybe something is missing?"

"Oh, shit."

I look over at Enzo who's staring hard at me. "Are you going through a midlife crisis or something?"

"No, I'm being serious." I hit the down button on the elevator. "Lately…I don't know. I've been really…unhappy."

"Why?" He looks truly puzzled. "You have everything you could ever want. Family, friends, money, a perfect brother."

When I don't say anything, a light suddenly dawns in his brown eyes.

"Aww, hell, this is about a woman, isn't it?"

"No. I'm not referring to a relationship." My response is too fast. "I don't let myself get close to women. Not emotionally, anyway."

We both can hear my unspoken words—*Not since Cynda.*

"Okay, nothing wrong with that. You're a busy man and will be even crazier busy once you start heading up the winery division. So, it sounds to me like you need to let off a little steam. Get laid."

The elevator dings and we step inside. "That's what I was thinking."

"Any prospects?"

"Unfortunately, no."

Enzo straightens his already perfect tie. "Maybe I can help with that."

"What do you mean?"

"There's a very private, extremely discrete event happening tonight. It would be the perfect place to pick up a woman for the evening. No strings attached."

"What event?" I ask.

"A private party of sorts," he answers, suddenly getting cagey.

I tilt my head, curious as hell. "Okaaay. Why aren't you going to this party if it's so great?"

"I have some more work to do and probably won't leave the office until late."

Damn, Enzo was a workaholic to the extreme. If anyone around here needed a vacation, it was him.

"But, if you're interested, I can give you my invite. Because you can't get in without one."

That last comment really piques my interest. "Is this some kind of illegal, underground—"

"No, nothing like that," he interrupts, and the elevator door glides open. We step out and he stops up short. "Well, I mean, not everything is exactly above board. But it's just all for entertainment purposes, right?" He shrugs a shoulder and starts walking again.

"What do you mean?"

We start walking through the lobby and now I'm downright perplexed. What is this mysterious event?

"Truthfully? I've been invited to this same party for the past three years and haven't ever gone. My time is precious and I rarely attend parties that don't involve shop talk and networking. But, I have heard rumors."

"What kind of rumors?"

"Just the usual," he answers evasively and motions for me to step through the revolving door first. Pushing through, I wait for him to come out on the other side and, as he does, he reaches into his inside jacket pocket and pulls out a simple white envelope. "Here."

I take the formal envelope and turn it over, checking out the waxed seal imprinted with a lamb. *What the hell?* "You've never gone?"

"Nope. But, I hope you do. Go and have a few drinks. Enjoy yourself and let loose a little. Pick up a beautiful woman and fuck her sense-less. Then by the time Monday morning rolls around, your head will be clear and in the game, and you won't be all mopey because you haven't had sex in the past year."

"That's not true!" My brow creases as it occurs to me Enzo is right. *Holy fuck.* It has been a whole year. Actually, more like one year and three months.

"C'mon, Vin, we all know you rarely let the little guy out to play." I glare at Enzo and he tosses his head back and laughs. His gaze drops to my crotch. "He's suffocating in there."

"Fuck you."

Enzo slaps a hand on my shoulder. "Go to the party tonight and have fun. The little guy and I are begging you."

Shrugging his hand away, I look down at the tempting invitation in my hand and say, "He's bigger than yours, bro."

And Enzo laughs even louder. "Yeah, right."

I keep looking at the strange seal. "What's up with the lamb? Kind of weird, don't you think?"

But Enzo only shrugs. "No clue."

I know that lambs represent innocence and purity. Seems a little odd that they'd stamp their invitations with the animal.

"I have heard some people refer to it as the White Auction, though. Whatever the hell that means," he offers.

Again, another symbol of purity.

"Okay, gotta go. And I'm going to want details all about the hot babe you picked up!"

"Yeah, sure," I respond and roll my eyes.

I watch my brother toss me a salute—we all do that for some reason—and head toward his expensive sports car parked up front near the door. God, that guy gets away with so much shit. *How did it not get towed?* I wonder, tucking the invite into my jacket pocket.

As I walk up the block, heading toward my apartment which is within walking distance, I feel the invitation burning a hole in my pocket. Even though exclusive, uppity parties aren't usually my scene, I'm seriously tempted to go. And, the closer I get to home, the more I'm leaning toward actually attending. Maybe it's exactly what I need— one night, no strings. And, hell, an end to my drought. Because, I can't deny it—my poor dick would like to have some fun tonight.

3

HANNAH

My feet are throbbing and, by the time I reach the convenience store, the kids have taken off. I grab the door, pull and it doesn't open. Glancing up, I see the "closed" sign hanging right in front of me and my heart drops sickeningly. *Dammit. Now what am I going to do?*

Spinning around, I race away from the store and risk a look over my shoulder. The behemoth is still chasing me down and he's getting way too close for comfort. My stupid shoes pinch my feet with every step and a fear like I've never known before washes over me. I don't see any people on the street and panic rises up hard and fast. Whipping around a corner, I figure my best bet is to duck between a couple of dark houses and lose him. Then I can backtrack, go over to my neighbor's place and call the police from there.

Unfortunately, things don't always work out the way you plan.

It takes me a second to realize my pursuer is no longer behind me. The thump of his boots is gone and I pause, breathing hard, and lean a hand against the side of the house. Where did he go? Did he give up?

Is he heading back to his car? Did I manage to outsmart him? Or, maybe I tired him out?

Completely frozen, too terrified to move, I listen to the sounds of the night. Listen for him. Pulling in a steadying breath, I creep forward and peer around the corner...

And he comes charging at me from out of the darkness!

A scream rips from my throat and I turn to run, but he grabs me around the waist and hauls me right up off my feet. Kicking and thrashing, I try to break free, but it's like trying to escape two steel bands wrapped around me. His grip is so tight, and I can barely breathe much less escape.

"Stop fighting," he growls into my ear, tightening his hold.

His voice is a raspy, scary hiss and I instantly stop struggling and do the complete opposite—go entirely slack in his arms, catching him off-guard. With a curse, he shifts his hold and then throws me over his shoulder like a sack of potatoes.

Facing the ground, I bounce against his wide back as he rounds the corner. I keep my eyes peeled, though, looking for a pedestrian or someone I can yell to for help, but no one is around. Just my bad luck.

My kidnapper sticks to the shadows and it doesn't take him long to reach an SUV parked at the curb. He carelessly tosses me into the back seat and I scramble up, surveying my surroundings. Somehow, I need to figure out a way to escape.

The car has blacked-out windows and, even though I know they're locked, I try pulling on the door handle. Okay, so there's no way out of this vehicle. Once we get to wherever we're headed, maybe I can try to make a run for it once he lets me out.

Squeezing my hands into fists, I bury my fear and force my brain to focus on a solution, a way out. There has to be something I can do. Just giving up isn't who I am. I've always been a fighter and I will go down fighting. But, I'm also a realist and my prospects look decidedly grim.

Figuring my best option is to wait it out, I hang tight, keeping a close eye on where we're going. There isn't much traffic and it's not long before the SUV pulls up in front of a hotel. Frowning, I wait until the back door opens and I come face to face with my stone-faced kidnapper. God, he's huge. Tilting my chin up, I stare right back at him, refusing to be intimidated or back down.

Behemoth lets out a snort then motions for me to get out. Slowly sliding off the seat, I keep one eye on him while quickly accessing my options. Sadly, I don't really have any. Except make a run for it, so that's what I do. As if he's expecting it, my kidnapper grabs me in a lightning-fast move and jerks me back next to him.

"Nice try," he grumbles then yanks me toward the front door of the hotel.

Hope rekindles and I know there must be employees inside. I could call out to them and they'll help me, right?

Wrong.

It only takes a minute to realize that the two employees at the front desk aren't going to do a thing to help me. They ignore my call and pretend like they don't even see me. Clearly, they're in on whatever is going on here. Or, more than likely, they've been paid off to ignore anything suspicious. Like a damsel in distress.

And this huge man dragging me into the elevator against my will is certainly classified as suspicious.

"Give it up, little girl," Behemoth states. "It's game over for you."

My stomach twists with dread. "You're taking me to Creed, aren't you?"

"You owe him a lot of money."

Well, he's right about that. There's no point in talking to Creed's minion any further, so I wait until I'm face to face with the loan shark himself. Once we reach the penthouse and step out of the elevator, I get to see Dexter Creed up close and personal for the first time. And he's just as intimidating as I would've guessed. Maybe even more so.

Creed's gaze slithers down my body and I try not to cringe. "Well, this is a pleasant surprise. I have to say, I'm glad you didn't have the money to just pay off your debt, Miss Everson. Meeting you in person is a nice surprise."

I swallow down the nasty retort on the tip of my tongue, but my eyes narrow. I hate this man already. It's my own fault, though. Instead of researching him and the miraculous check that seemed to appear out of nowhere, I didn't question anything. I ran to the bank, cashed it as quickly as possible and paid for my mom's care. With hindsight, I suppose I would've done the exact same thing. My mom's comfort and care, especially in her final days, was the most important thing in the world to me. Okay, I'm in a shitload of trouble now, but at least I can say I did everything within my power to make sure my mom was taken care of.

So, yeah, zero regrets.

But now it's time to pay the piper. Or, in this case, Dexter Creed.

While Creed studies me, I scope him out right back. His sparse, blond hair is slicked back off his face and he sports a thin mustache. The look suits him, reminding me of a weasel. Slick, smart and quick. And, definitely not to be trusted. When he gives me a smarmy smile, I try not to grimace.

"You're younger than I thought you'd be." Once again, his attention roams over me and I do my best to ignore the creepiness factor skittering down my spine. "How old are you, Hannah?"

I lift my chin. "Twenty-two," I state, keeping my voice firm and steady even though on the inside, I'm quaking. Like a leaf in a windstorm.

But I don't want him to know that.

"Spirited, too. I like that." He takes a step closer, but I don't back down. "Fearless. Although, you should be very afraid of me, little one."

I don't respond, just stare straight into his pale blue eyes. Now, instead of a weasel, I'm getting snake vibes. That empty look in his gaze is unsettling. I'm about to move away when he chuckles softly.

"Maybe I should keep you for myself."

"What?" My jaw drops and I wonder if I misheard him.

But he ignores me. "You owe me quite a nice chunk of change. Can you pay me back?"

I clear my throat. "I can pay you back...if you'll be kind enough to allow a payment plan. I just need a little more time and I know we can work something out if—"

"I don't do payment plans." His mouth edges up in a sneer. "So, here's the deal, Hannah, and I suggest you listen very closely. You have two choices. One, my guy here breaks your arm then returns in three days to collect the money. If you still don't have it, he's going to break your other arm. That process will continue with your legs. Once there's nothing left to break...well, I'm sure you can guess what happens."

Shit. My stomach sinks because there's no way I can pay him back within that short amount of time. I'd need months, years even. "What's the other option?" I whisper, even though I have a feeling I'd rather not know.

"Choice two is easy and will clear your debt by morning."

My ears perk up. By morning? How is that possible?

"Are you still a virgin, Hannah?"

Oh, God. Bile crawls up the back of my throat. "I don't see what that has to do with anything."

"It has everything to do with what I'm about to propose."

One night in his bed. It has to be that and there's no way in hell I'd sleep with this vile man. I'd rather have my arms and legs broken.

"Tonight at midnight, I'm hosting an auction. But to participate, you must have something extremely valuable to auction off. Something a man will pay an exorbitant and indecent amount of money to obtain."

The pieces begin to click. This piece of shit wants me to auction off my virginity.

"I think that sweet cherry of yours will bring me much more than you owe me. So, as tempting as it is to keep you for myself..." His gaze skates down my body again and I swallow back the vomit, "I'd rather have the cold, hard cash."

A thousand thoughts fly through my head and I need to handle the situation with Creed carefully. If I agree to sell my virginity to the highest bidder, my debt will be paid. Done. No looking over my shoulder and running again. Quick and easy.

But, I don't think I could sleep with a complete stranger. I haven't been saving myself, but the opportunity to have sex hasn't really presented itself, either. I've been too busy working and taking care of my mother. Dating and men have been the last thing on my mind.

Could I close my eyes and just go through the motions? A shiver runs through me. It would be awful and humiliating. Not to mention awkward and painful.

"Well? I don't have all night. Yes or no?" he asks coldly.

Despite being scared out of my mind to give my virginity to a total stranger, I should just agree right now and, in the meantime, come up with an escape plan. I need to buy some time. "Okay," I relent softly. "If you promise to clear my debt then...I'll do it. I'll auction off my virginity."

It kills me to say the words, but I'll be damned before I actually go through with it. My options are extremely slim right now and Creed knows that.

"Good. And, yes, that will erase what you owe me." He turns to his goon and orders him to take me to room 222. "Go freshen up and make yourself presentable. There's an outfit in the closet you can wear during the auction."

As I turn to leave, racking my brain for a plan, I hear Creed's final words.

"Wise decision, Hannah. I would've hated destroying a creature as lovely as you."

Completely revolted, I follow Behemoth, ignoring Creed who laughs as I walk out. The giant escorts me to a hotel room on the second floor and then nods for me to go inside. Once I step into the room, I shut the door and see there's no security latch. *Dammit.* A quick look through the peephole tells me Behemoth isn't going anywhere. He's standing guard right outside my door. *Great. How the hell am I going to escape?*

I hurry over and drag the curtains open. The windows are securely latched and the drop is too far to chance a jump. A quick glance around tells me I'm stuck in here.

"Shit," I whisper. What the hell am I going to do? At this point, it seems like my only option is to get ready and then once I'm at the auction, I can try to run away. That's really cutting it close, though, and there's always the possibility I might not be able to escape. Being sold to a man like chattel makes me sick. Having my arms and legs broken also doesn't sit well with me.

If it comes down to it, can I do it? Can I sleep with a stranger? I suppose I could let my mind float somewhere else and how long is it really going to last, anyway? Ten minutes? Realistically, it will be a small amount of time to sacrifice. I'm tough. If necessary, I can suck it up, spread my legs and pray he's gentle. Whoever the pervert is who buys a young girl's virginity.

Eww.

I suppose I should get ready. If I'm going to have to do this, if there's truly no other way out, then I want to at least look good enough that someone will bid. It is an auction, after all, and I can't imagine the humiliation I'd feel if no one wanted me.

Walking over to the closet, I open the door and want to cry when I see the "outfit" I'm supposed to wear. It's nothing more than a wispy piece of lingerie. Silky sheer, predictably white and with lace embroidered edges.

I can't believe I'm going to do this. How has my life come to this?

Heart pounding madly, I lay the lingerie on the bed, drop down on the edge of the mattress and cry. Cry my eyes out until there's nothing left to do except wash my face, get dressed and suck it up.

4

VIN

I spend the entire evening debating whether or not I should go to the private party tonight. *The White Auction.* Eventually, my libido wins over everything else. I need to get fucking laid. I'm sick of my brothers teasing me about it and I'm wound so damn tight, I'm ready to pop.

Since Enzo never went to one of these parties, I have no idea what to expect. I figure I should be okay if I wear black pants with my green button down dress shirt. I like the shirt because it makes my green eyes pop. I'm the only one of my siblings who has eyes that aren't brown, so they always used to joke that I'm not really a Rossi and my dad was the mailman.

Leaning over the bathroom sink, I spritz a small amount of cologne on and study my reflection. My thick brown hair waves back from my sun-bronzed face and my lower jaw is covered in a light stubble. My green eyes look brighter than usual and resemble twin emeralds.

"You are going to meet a beautiful woman tonight and end this dry spell," I tell myself, trying to be positive.

With that goal firmly set in my mind, I hit the light off and walk out into the living room. Grabbing my wallet, I double check there's a condom still in there—yep, still mocking me—and snap the leather billfold shut, tucking it in my back pocket.

After swiping up the invitation with the odd wax seal, I grab my jacket and head down to the elevator. I live on the twenty-second floor of Skyview Towers. I could've bought a place higher up, but the truth is I don't care for heights that much. Living on the eightieth floor is the last place I want to be and twenty two is high enough for me. Heights make me edgy. Unlike Angelo who loves soaring around in his helo, I prefer to keep my feet on the ground. Or, as close to the ground as possible.

The elevator drops me off in the underground garage and I walk over to my Mercedes. The address on the invitation is about twenty minutes away. Surprisingly, traffic moves fairly well and I arrive at the hotel a little after midnight. I don't want to look too eager, but I am not playing around tonight. The goal is to scope the place out, find a willing woman and get the hell out of here. Since we'll already be in a hotel that makes it super convenient.

I pull right up to the front door and valet park my car. As I walk up the steps and enter the hotel, I realize it's packed. *Are all these people here for the private party?* I wonder. A woman is directing people to a doorway where two men are checking invitations. Pulling mine out, I remove it from the pristine white envelope and present it to one of the men. He scans a special light over it then hands it back to me.

"Welcome, Mr. Rossi. Help yourself to champagne and hor d'oeuvres. The auction begins at 12:30 sharp."

Huh. So there actually is a real auction? Enzo didn't know any specific details, but maybe they have some artwork on display or something, and they plan to donate the earnings to a local charity. Most parties like this are full of wealthy people who want to feel better about themselves and like to open their wallet for a good cause. There's only one reason I'm opening my wallet tonight—and that's to remove that condom, blow off the dust and fuck a lovely lady.

Christ, I can't wait. Enzo was right. I need some action.

A heavy, red velvet curtain hangs in front of me and I push through it. The moment I step into the next room, a pretty girl offers me a glass of champagne. Taking it from the tray, I murmur a thanks and look around. I don't see any artwork on display, but I do see a platform that looks like it's going to serve as some kind of a stage. Maybe they'll present the auction items up there a little later. Honestly, I don't care. Chances are, if I can move this little search along, I might manage to make it out of here before the action even begins.

Now, though, it's time to scope things out. I take a sip of champagne and begin making my way around the room. Disappointment shreds me because there are a helluva lot more men here than women. And the women I do see already seem to be with someone.

There's also a weird vibe I'm picking up on. Almost one of anticipation. I'm not sure why people would be so excited to bid on a painting, but whatever. To each his own, right?

Telling myself to be patient, I find a quiet corner away from the crowd and study everyone closely. Looks like a lot of single businessmen, some couples, and no single women. I swear to God, if this evening turns out to be a bust, I'm going to be pissed. My hopes—and the little guy's hopes—are up. It would suck ass if there aren't any single, eligible women who show up.

Patience, Vin. You're going to meet someone tonight.

After people-watching for almost twenty-five minutes and finding no prospects, I accept another glass of champagne and consider heading out. As I'm debating what to do, a man walks up onto the raised platform in the center of the room. He looks quite theatrical and wears a suit with tails along with a tophat and holds a walking stick with a sparkling crystal on its top. If I didn't know better, I'd say he stepped right out of *Moulin Rouge* which is currently playing over on Broadway.

"Welcome to the White Auction, ladies and gentlemen. We have anything you could possibly want. Your heart's desire" he assures the crowd who suddenly comes to life, completely animated and bursting with enthusiasm. I can feel the wave of anticipation building. "So many delights to bid on. Keep in mind, all bidding begins at five-thousand dollars. Now, let's start the show!"

Leaning my shoulder against the wall, I watch as a young girl walks up onto the stage.

"This is Violet, but I promise you she's not shy. In fact, she likes company, preferably in three's, if you know what I mean," the announcer says and people laugh, moving closer to the platform, watching the girl. She's wearing a short skirt and does a little dance, shaking her ass. That's when the bids start rolling in. Men yell out numbers and the more she flaunts herself, the more money they offer.

What in the actual fuck? With a deep frown, I keep watching, unable to look away. It's like a train wreck that's about to happen and, even though I know I should just walk away, I can't. The girl bends over and flashes her ass to the room. Stifling a sigh, I listen to the final few offers and it becomes quite clear she's offering herself for a *ménage à trois.*

"Bam! Twenty-thousand dollars is our top bid. Violet belongs to you for the night, my lovelies."

Some couple struts over, each takes one of Violet's hands and helps her walk down the stairs and out the door.

Lovely. I roll my eyes and ignore the disgust rising inside me, sharp and bitter like bile up the back of my throat. I don't like to judge people. If they're not hurting anyone then do whatever makes you happy. But, this right here isn't my scene and I'm certainly not about to pay for sex.

I'm leaning against the wall, unable to look away, when twins parade onto the stage. The bidding erupts and I watch grown men scream out bids, fighting over these two young women. In the end, some skeezy guy in a rumpled suit walks to the end of the dais and gleefully rubs his hands together as the twins join him. They giggle and then disappear into the crowd of people.

Oh, for fuck's sake. This is clearly some kind of weird sex auction and I'll be damned before I pay to sleep with one of these women auctioning their bodies off. Pulling my phone out of my pocket, I call Enzo as another woman parades onto the stage, flashing her tits to the audience who immediately lets out raucous hoots and whistles.

"Why're you calling me when you're supposed to be having hot sex with a stranger?" Enzo says in greeting.

"I don't pay for sex," I hiss into the phone. "What the hell kind of party is this?"

Enzo laughs. "How would I know? I told you I never went. But call me intrigued. What exactly is going on?"

"I could kill you, you know that?" He chuckles and I roll my eyes. "So, there's this raised platform in the center of the room and this man dressed like some kind of weird *Moulin Rouge* character is auctioning off another girl as we speak. Bidding starts at five-thousand bucks and I guess the winner gets a night with their prize."

"Ah, explains why they wanted a credit card on file," Enzo murmurs. "Girls or women? Do they look legal?"

"Yeah, I'm pretty sure they're at least eighteen. Well, from what I've seen so far, anyway." His last comment has me frowning. "You gave them a credit card number?"

"I can't remember. But now I'm thinking I must have. Huh. Maybe I should've gone to this."

"It's a damn meat market and not my scene. The first girl went for twenty grand. Who the hell is pocketing this money?"

"Good question. I honestly never looked into it. And, yeah, I was only kidding. Twenty grand is a bit much for a one-night stand. What's so special about these women? Do they come with a stock certificate or what?"

"I have no idea," I grumble. "But, I'm leaving."

"Sorry, bro," Enzo says sincerely. "I really thought you might be able to find somebody there."

"Yeah, not likely. Talk to you later." I hang up and, as I'm slipping my phone back into my pocket, another girl climbs up the stairs and moves beneath the spotlight. I'm about to head for the exit when I abruptly stop. I'm not sure what it is that captures my attention, but I pause mid-step and check out the newest piece of ass.

"Tonight, we have a very special young woman in our presence. Her name is…Mary…and it's quite fitting since our lovely, little lamb has quite a bit to offer."

Lamb. Purity…innocence…my heart sinks at the look on her face. It's fear.

All of my attention zeroes in on the young woman standing in the middle of the stage. She's wearing a thin white negligee that's danger-ously close to being sheer. With the light shining behind her, I can see straight through the bottom of her short nightgown and the outline of her slim thighs is clear. Her long blonde hair frames her angelic-looking face and it almost seems to glow. Kind of all gold and radiant like she has a halo surrounding her.

Despite standing tall and proud, I can't miss the panicked look in her eyes and when I glance down at her hands, I swear they're shaking. Unlike the other girls who paraded across the stage, willingly strutting their stuff, Mary just stands there looking like an angel in headlights.

If I didn't know better, I'd say she doesn't want to be up there. My chest tightens, heart twisting at the vulnerable look on her face. *Is someone forcing her to do this?* The thought makes me feel sick. I also have the overwhelming urge to reach out and help her off that damn stage.

"The bidding for our little virgin will start at ten grand." He chuckles as the crowd erupts in a frenzy.

Virgin? Oh, hell, no.

"I'm sure you all understand why our little lamb is worth more than the rest. So let the bidding begin, you sinners! Who wants our sweet, little, *innocent* Mary?"

The sound of frantic bids fill the air and I walk closer, unable to look away from the little martyr on stage. The closer I get, the more clearly I can see her. And the fear in her pretty blue eyes is clearly evident. Especially as the men fighting over her grow more determined, more intense.

The bidding hits thirty grand fast, the highest of the night so far, and my gut twists. A group of men are going back and forth, each trying to outbid the other, and it makes me want to go over there and beat the shit out of them all. Can't they see she's scared? That she doesn't want to be up on that fucking platform, practically naked in front of all these strangers?

My protector instinct flares to life, kicking in hard, and I decide she isn't going to any of these idiots. They're all up close to the stage now, salivating like a pack of feral dogs, eyes gleaming brightly with the idea of debauching that poor girl.

"Thirty-five grand," the one man declares and glares triumphantly at his opponent who doesn't offer a new bid.

"Thirty-six grand," a voice says and I look over and see a man in a suit who looks vaguely familiar. He has a smug look on his face that I don't like, as if he knows he's going to walk away the winner tonight. *Hmm. We'll see about that.*

I step up to the stage and say loudly, "Fifty-thousand dollars."

Gasps fill the air and the angel on the stage turns her attention to me, jaw dropping open.

"We have a new bidder," the auctioneer announces excitedly. "And a very impressive bid of fifty-thousand dollars for the lovely Mary Mary quite contrary who I'm sure has a very lovely garden." He heckles out a laugh. "Why don't you give the men a peek at your garden?"

Mary, or whatever her real name is, looks horrified and takes an unsteady step back. I frown at her reaction and the auctioneer's perverse twist on the children's nursery rhyme. Then my attention moves to my opponent and I wait to see if he will try to outbid me.

"Fifty-one thousand," he snaps fast, glaring at me.

Here we go. I love a good challenge and he just laid one down. I play with him as he nickel and dimes the bid slowly up by one-thousand dollar increments. *Cheap bastard.* Is that all she's worth to him? A lousy 56K?

After that last bid, I send him a scathing look then turn to the auctioneer and in a loud, clear voice, I state, "One-hundred fifty six thousand dollars."

The crowd gasps, goes eerily quiet then bursts in raucous approval. They hoot and stomp their feet, and they whistle and clap wildly.

Beat that, asshole.

When he doesn't challenge my offer, I turn back to the auctioneer and he declares me the winner. Someone hands me an envelope, but I'm more concerned about getting Mary—or whatever her name really is —off that blasted stage and out of this goddamn room of vultures. She doesn't belong in here with these twisted people.

Her blue gaze meets mine and when I lift my hand up, offering it to her, she grasps onto it like I'm a rock in the storm currently tossing her around. As I help her walk down the steps, our gazes remain locked and it hits me hard that this poor girl is terrified. I can feel her shaking and before her small, bare feet can touch the floor, I sweep her up into my arms. Another cheer goes up from the crowd, but I ignore them and stalk out of the room, trying to get her away from all these deviant idiots as quickly as possible.

By the time I reach the elevator, she's trembling so damn hard. I tighten my arms around her. "It's okay," I assure her in a low voice. "I'm not going to hurt you."

I have no plans to take this young woman's virginity tonight. But the urge to get her up to the room where she'll be safe fills me.

She tilts her head up and stares at me with startling blue eyes. "Do you promise?" she asks.

"I promise," I whisper and step into the elevator.

5

HANNAH

My trembling subsides in the tall stranger's arms as we ride up in the elevator. That takes me completely off-guard because I'm expecting the fear to kick in harder as we get closer to his room. But, for some strange, inexplicable reason, this man feels like my rescuer, not my enemy. The other men who were fighting over winning me, on the other hand, were not good news and left me terrified. They had evil intentions. Of course, maybe I'm just in denial and hoping this man who I'm clinging to won't hurt me.

"It's okay. I'm not going to hurt you."

"Promise?"

"I promise."

Am I fool to believe him? Yes. But, I want his words to be true more than anything.

My fingers curl into his shirt, clutching at the soft cotton, and I find myself looking up to sneak a glance at his strong profile. Whoever he is, he's very handsome. Stubble covers his angular chin and he possesses high cheekbones and a straight, perfectly-shaped nose. His hair is thick and dark brown, shorter on the sides and longer on top, neatly swept back. And his eyes...simply stunning. Two bright green gems that suddenly look down and lock onto me. Very serious and full of...concern?

"Are you okay?" he asks, gaze searching my face.

I nod, unable to find the words to respond. They're caught in my throat. A part of me feels like I should tell him to put me down, but I don't want that. I want him to hold me in his arms and never let go.

The elevator door slides open and he steps out.

"I'm going to set you down now, okay?" His voice is low, almost soothing, and I reluctantly let go of his shirt, realizing I wrinkled it from holding onto him so hard.

"Sorry," I whisper as my bare feet touch the carpet, "I got you all wrinkly." Without thinking, I reach up and try to smooth the material down, unable to miss his hard chest muscles and how they feel beneath my touch.

He pulls in a breath and freezes. "It's fine. Don't worry about it."

I nod and lower my hand, suddenly feeling foolish, and watch as he removes a keycard from an envelope and opens the door.

"Go ahead." He motions for me to go inside and my heart kicks up again. This man is a complete stranger and though it momentarily felt like he was saving me, should I be scared? Does he plan to use me tonight? Even though he told me he wasn't going to hurt me, can I trust him? Doubt fills me and I hesitate.

Then it hits me hard—this man just paid one-hundred and fifty six thousand dollars to spend the night with me. Of course, he's going to want something in return. Why else would he have forked out a fortune? My feet refuse to move and he looks down at me with those amazing emerald eyes.

"What's wrong?" he asks.

Once again, words elude me. I clear my throat and cross my arms over my chest. The silkiness of the negligee reminds me that I'm standing here, wearing practically nothing.

"If you come inside," he murmurs softly, "I can give you my jacket. And we can order some room service if you're hungry."

His kindness touches me and emotion crashes over me. Lowering my face, I move past him and enter the room as tears threaten to fall. The last couple of weeks have been an emotional rollercoaster and I'm not sure how much more I can take. I've never felt so lost or alone in my entire life. Standing in the middle of the room, not sure what to do, I turn and watch him close the door. Then he shrugs his jacket off and holds it open for me. I take a tentative step closer and let him slip it over my shoulders. It's so warm and smells really good—a little citrusy, and a lot masculine. Pulling his jacket tighter around me, I look up and see him watching me closely. There's nothing in his expression that scares me or makes me wary; his bright green eyes are strangely calming and, if I'm not mistaken, hold a touch of sympathy. Or, maybe it's empathy.

"Sit," he murmurs, and I drop down on the edge of the bed. "Can we talk?"

"You just paid a ton of money for my company. I think that can be arranged."

A laugh bursts from his throat. "I did, didn't I?" Then he grows serious again, studying me closely. "You didn't belong up on that stage. I would've paid more to get you out of there."

My eyes widen and it occurs to me that he's serious. "Why?" I ask, voice barely a whisper. Who is this amazing man? And why did he come to my rescue?

His face darkens at my question. "Because I didn't like the way those men were fighting over you. Like you were some prize they could win. There's no way I was letting any of them walk out of there with you."

"But, why?" I ask again, thoroughly confused. "As much as I appreciate your help, you don't even know me. And, you certainly don't owe me anything."

He slowly lowers down on the mattress beside me. "Correct me if I'm wrong, but I had the impression you didn't want to be up there."

"No, I didn't."

"How did you wind up on that stage?"

I pull in a shaky breath and think over the hell my life has been this past month. Before I can stop myself, it all pours out of me—my mom being sick, how I was unable to pay for her treatments and provide her with the level of care I wanted, and how my desperation made me accept a loan from Dexter Creed.

"I made a deal with the devil," I say, "and when he came to collect, I didn't have the money to pay him back. So his enforcer brought me back here and Creed told me I could basically have every bone in my body broken before he killed me or…"

"Or you could participate in the auction," he finishes, disgust lacing his deep voice.

I nod. "And then my debt would be paid off. Quickly and completely, and I wouldn't have to worry about running any longer."

"Your virginity was a steep price to pay."

Lowering my head, I clasp and unclasp my hands nervously. "I know. But better than dying, right?" I give him a half-hearted smile. "I'm just lucky you were there. I'll never be able to pay you back."

His knuckles brush along my jaw and he tilts my chin up. "It's all taken care of and all I ask is one thing."

Uh oh. Here it comes. The real reason he paid all that money and swept me out of there. Swallowing hard, I look into his deep, green eyes. "What?" I manage to force out.

"What's your name? I highly doubt it's Mary," he adds dryly.

My name? Frowning in confusion, I wait for him to demand something more in return, but he doesn't. He just looks at me expectantly. "Um, it's Hannah," I tell him. "Hannah Everson."

"It's nice to meet you, Hannah. I'm Vin Rossi."

"Vin?" I echo. "As in Vincent?"

He shakes his head. "No. Vincentius. But, nobody calls me that— except my mom."

Vin gives me an adorable lopsided grin and my stomach dips precariously. He's so good-looking and it's a little discombobulating. Yet something about him puts me at ease. "When you're in trouble?" I ask, a small smile curving my mouth upward.

"Exactly."

For a long moment, we just look at each other, smiling, and then his attention dips, focusing a moment too long on my lips. Without meaning to, I lick them and he clears his throat and shifts his attention over to the table where the room service menu lays.

"How about some food?" he suggests.

I'm sure the prices are outrageous and I hesitate.

"My treat," he quickly adds.

"Oh, no, I couldn't—"

"I insist." His tone is firm and brooks no argument.

Now that the influx of adrenaline has worn off, I am hungry. I can't remember the last time I ate. Other than a glass of Coke and half a bagel at the diner during my break, I haven't eaten since yesterday. "Okay, thank you," I whisper.

"What do you have a taste for?" He flips the pages and I pull my feet up onto the bed, tucking them beneath me.

"Anything."

"You gotta give me more than that. Cheeseburger, fries, salad, pizza, steak?"

"A grilled cheese and french fries sound good," I tell him, feeling shy all of a sudden. "Oh, and a Coke."

"Done."

I sit back and listen as he places the order, watching the way his throat moves as he talks and how his large hand holds the phone to his ear. His fingers are long and elegant-looking. The green button down shirt he's wearing fits his broad shoulders perfectly, pulling a little, and I can't help but notice the way the material hugs his muscled arms. Or, the way the color makes his amazing green eyes pop. My gaze tracks downward over his torso, and the shirt is tucked into a pair of nice, black dress pants. When I realize I'm looking at his crotch, I pull my lower lip into my mouth, and move my eyes downward to his thick, muscled thighs. My goodness, his legs are long and I swallow hard.

Vincentius Rossi is every woman's dream man. Suddenly, I'm so damn curious about my savior. After he hangs up, I tilt my head and meet those incredible green eyes of his. "How old are you?" I ask bluntly.

"Thirty-two," he answers without hesitation. "How about you?"

Oh, I didn't expect him to be so much older. Although, I should've known. He's very refined and mature. "I'm twenty-two."

Vin coughs behind his hand and moves away from me slightly. I wonder if I just freaked him out. Ten years is a lot, but I'm not a minor or anything. Not that it matters. We're just up here and going to eat dinner. That's all.

That's all. Right?

"I don't think I thanked you properly," I say and his head whips over. "Thank you...so very much. Tonight could've ended...well, very badly for me."

"You don't have to thank me. Creed is a disgusting human being to make you do that."

"Can I ask you a question?" He nods. "Why were you at the auction? It doesn't seem like your scene."

"It's not," he quickly replies. "My brother gave me the invite. He had no idea what it was about. He just thought it was a party and that I needed to, ah, get out and have some fun."

"Oh, I see." I look down at my fingernail and pick at the chipped, pink polish. "Can I ask you something else?"

"You can ask me anything you want if it makes you feel more comfortable," he tells me, face so serious that any lingering fear seems to melt away.

"Are we spending the night here? Or are you going to take me home?"

He seems to be considering my question carefully before answering. "I think we should stay here until morning. Just in case anyone is keeping tabs."

"Why would they keep tabs?"

He shrugs a shoulder. "Honestly, they probably aren't, but I don't know how this whole thing works and if we leave early, it might draw attention. And I don't want you back in the spotlight for any reason. I'd much rather we lay low for the rest of the night, stay under the radar, and leave bright and early. Is that okay with you?"

"I think so," I answer quietly.

"You can trust me, Hannah. I know you have no reason to, but I won't hurt you. I swear it."

I want to tell him that I believe him and trust in his promise, but the words feel like glue in my mouth, all stuck together and unable to come out. He's a stranger and I don't trust easily. Plus, I keep remembering how much money he paid for me. How can anyone just be able to afford to throw that amount of money away and not even blink?

"Are you really rich?" I blurt out. I probably sound rude and I instantly backtrack. "Sorry."

His mouth edges up and I shift on the bed, trying to find the right words.

"I'm just having a hard time wrapping my head around the fact you basically flushed all that money down the toilet. Yet, you don't seem to care at all."

"First off, I think that money went to a very good cause. Don't you?"

"I guess so," I say slowly.

"And, second, to answer your question—yes, I have enough money that it doesn't matter."

"Oh," I whisper. He must be a millionaire. "Can I ask what you do?"

"My family owns a very prosperous vineyard in Sicily and I'm in charge of running the American division headquartered here in New York."

My brows go up. "Wow. That sounds like a very important job. I can see why you get paid the big bucks."

Vin barks out a laugh. "Well, if I'm being completely honest, I'm technically not starting my new position as president until Monday morning."

"Are you excited?"

AVA GRAY

He shrugs a shoulder. "Excited isn't the right word. But, I look forward to having something to do."

I'm not sure when I became so curious, but I can't stop asking this man questions. "Do you get to visit Sicily a lot?"

"I go back at least a couple of times a year. My parents still live on the island."

"Oh, that must be nice. I've never been there." I tilt my head, studying his dark Italian good looks. The man is ridiculously attractive and when he looks at me with those stunning green eyes, my ovaries flutter. "Can you speak Italian?"

He nods then leans closer and says a string of beautiful, foreign words in his deep, low, intoxicating voice. And, if my ovaries fluttered before? Now, they just burst. Holy hell, hearing him speak in Italian is so freaking sexy. For a moment, I'm not sure how to respond.

"What did you say?" I finally manage to ask, feeling more than a little flustered.

He sends me a panty-melting smile. "I said I'm glad you're safe, in here with me and, despite the earlier circumstances, I'm happy that we have this time to get to know each other better."

"Ohh." My heart does a weird little flip-flop in my chest and, when I switch my position on the mattress, there's no denying it. My panties are wet.

Before I can say anything else, our food arrives. The moment I get a whiff of it, my stomach growls in anticipation. Vin tips the server then carries two covered plates over to the bed. I pull the lid off and breathe deeply. A grilled cheese and fries never looked so good. I grab a half, sink my teeth into the gooey deliciousness and and moan with undisguised delight and appreciation. "This is the best grilled cheese I've ever had. Thank you, Vin." He pauses before biting into his hamburger and has the oddest look on his face. "What?"

"Nothing," he murmurs and takes a bite, watching me closely as he chews.

It doesn't take me long to devour my sandwich and attack my fries. Swiping one through a pile of ketchup, I munch happily, studying my savior. And, to my surprise and delight, he's studying me right back. Caught staring at each other, we both smile and my face instantly flushes.

"So, Hannah, what do you do? Are you in school?"

I shake my head. "No, I work at a diner."

He stops chewing and swallows the food down. "Do you like it?"

"No, I hate being on my feet all day. But I tell myself I'm lucky to have a job because not everyone does, right?"

"Right," he says slowly. "I suppose that's a good way to look at it."

But, for whatever reason, he doesn't look happy to learn where I work.

"So, what else do you do?" I ask, wanting to learn more about the man who rescued me tonight and then fed me dinner with zero expectations other than a friendly chat.

"My brothers and I run the other family businesses."

"Businesses?" I echo and take a sip of my Coke. *Wow.* He must have a ton of money. I'm not surprised, though. Vin Rossi looks like the kind of man who sits behind a big desk in a corner office in some fancy highrise. He exudes a calm, cool control that I find fascinating and I'm pretty willing to bet he knows how to handle just about any situation with aplomb.

He nods, but he doesn't go into any details. I've never been able to talk so freely with a man before and, for whatever reason, Vin makes me feel safe and secure. And that's something I haven't felt in a very long time. Hell, maybe ever. I've always been the one taking care of my mom and making sure everything was done. So it's really nice to have someone look out for me.

Stifling a yawn, I set my empty plate aside.

"Tired?" Vin asks.

"Exhausted," I admit. "It's been a long...I would say day, but it's been more like a long few months."

"I'm sure. And I'm sorry about your mother."

"Thank you," I whisper. "She was my best friend."

Once again, his knuckles caress along my jawline and then his hand moves to cup my chin. "You're going to be okay, Hannah. From now on, everything is going to be okay. I promise."

"Why do you care?" I can't help but ask the question.

"I don't know," he answers honestly and shrugs. "But, I do."

I'm not sure how long we stare at each other before I say, "Can I ask you another question."

He nods.

"Why did you spend so much money to buy me—er, my virginity— and you don't want to sleep with me?"

His green eyes darken a shade. "I never said I don't want to sleep with you," he says in a low, gruff voice and my pulse thunders madly in my ears. "But I won't take something that isn't freely given. And I've never paid for sex."

"Oh," I simply say, not sure how exactly to respond to that. Then, before I even realize what's happening, Vin leans in and lightly presses his lips against mine. The kiss is over before I can even process it.

"Go to sleep, Hannah," Vin says softly. "You're safe."

When he pulls his hand away, I immediately miss its warmth. With a nod, I scoot backwards and crawl under the covers. I don't even have the energy to go to the bathroom. Even though I'm in a hotel room with a complete stranger, it only takes me a few minutes to fall asleep. Because some part of me knows that I can trust Vin with my life, that he'd never harm me. Only protect me. *My savior.*

At some point, the mattress beside me sinks and I know he's lying down, too. And, I've never felt so very safe or slept so soundly in my entire life.

6

VIN

For the first time in a long time, I sleep comfortably all night beside a woman. It's been a long time since that's happened. Since Cynda. Before she broke my heart, anyway. Pushing thoughts of that traitor aside, I open my eyes and turn onto my side to watch the angel still sleeping beside me.

Because that's exactly what she looks like. Hannah's long, blonde hair is spread all over the pillow, surrounding her like a golden pool, and I'm tempted to reach out and touch a silky strand. Long, black lashes practically sweep across her high cheekbones and her full, pink lips look soft and, God help me, so damn kissable.

I shouldn't have kissed her last night. Not that it was much of a kiss, but I did press my lips to hers briefly and, dammit, it was more memorable than any kiss I've had within the last five years. Thinking about it, even though it had been completely innocent, makes my body react. *Shit.* I tell myself to shut it down, to ignore the lust rising within me and, instead, I focus on the innocent woman sleeping so close I can smell her baby powder scent.

Hannah Everson is beautiful. It's not something I can ignore. She's also sweet and trusting. I have an unexplainable and all-consuming urge to take care of her. I don't want her returning to some dumpy apartment and low-paying job where she has to stand on her feet all day. Instead, I want to sweep her off to my luxury apartment, tuck her into my king-size bed and worship her. I want to give her gifts and money and make her life easy. I'd also like to give her pleasure. So much pleasure that her body would writhe and she'd cry out my name.

I know I'm not going to ever give my heart away again. Having it crushed once was enough and I promised myself that I would never allow myself to be vulnerable like I was with Cynda. But, I could still have Hannah in my life, couldn't I? A girlfriend or wife isn't an option. However, I'm open to a lover. Wide fucking open. When I look at Hannah, I know I have to be careful, though. She's young, tempting and could fuck my heart up big-time if I were to be stupid enough to open it up again.

But that isn't going to happen, though. I can handle a beautiful woman in my bed. Make her my mistress, my lover. I just have to make sure my feelings don't extend beyond that. Protecting my heart is paramount. I refuse to be made a fool of again by a woman I thought I loved and trusted. No fucking way. It's not a chance I'll ever take again.

Hearts, love and all that bullshit are off the table. Sex, fucking and gifts are what I'm thinking. What I can handle.

But, can she?

Hannah's lips part and a soft breath escapes. Her face looks so soft and at ease while she sleeps. I could watch her forever. I'm not sure what it is about her that draws me in so completely. Her innocence? Her smile? Her beauty? Her intelligence? God knows, she is the full package.

Speaking of packages...

I stifle a groan and flip onto my back, ignoring the way my morning wood tents the sheet. *Fuck me.* It's more than that, though. Whether she realizes it or not, Hannah Everson has unleashed a shitload of feelings and sensations in me. Emotions that I thought were long-dead and never to return. To be honest, I'm not sure how I feel about it, either. It scares me, excites me...makes me want to jump up and down and ask her out on a date.

Rolling my head, I look over at her and wonder if she'd like to go to dinner with me. Ten years is a pretty decent age gap, but nothing too crazy, right? I'm only thirty-two not sixty-two. I'm just glad I was able to pay off the money she owed to that asshole Dexter Creed. Now that he has what he wants, there's no reason he should be sending his goons to harass her any further. She should be completely out of danger.

Hannah's eyes flutter open a moment later and her baby blues look slightly confused, as if she can't remember where she is or why I'm here. Then the edge of her mouth lifts in a half-smile.

"Good morning," I say.

"Good morning." She stretches like a very satisfied feline and my attention drops to the white negligee. She's a tiny thing, but her luscious breasts press against the silky material and I force myself to look away. Squeezing my eyes shut, I suppress a groan and try not to picture the light pink, dusk-colored nipples that I just glimpsed. *Impossible.* The image is forever burned in my mind and my dick flares back to life.

Turning onto my side to hide my raging hard-on, I blurt out, "Can I take you out to dinner tonight?"

Smooth, I mentally chastise myself. *Real smooth, idiot.*

Surprise flashes across her face. "Really? I mean, yes, I'd like that." A blush steals over her cheeks.

I love how she gets shy all of a sudden and it takes every bit of my self-control not to drag her over and kiss her senseless. Hell, I'd like to do a lot more than that. I want to part those sweet thighs and kiss her lower lips until her juices cover my mouth and tongue. I want to lick and suck her clit until she's crying out in pleasure. Then I want to sink my cock deep inside her wet heat and make her come again. Make her scream my name.

Make her all mine. Only mine.

Pulling in a deep, steadying breath, I force myself to calm down. One thing at a time. "How's six o'clock?" I ask, my voice hoarse with need.

"Good." She sits up and pulls my jacket up and around her shoulders because it had slipped off. It's way too big, but I like it on her. Way more than I should.

"Good." She's looking at me like she can't quite believe we're in bed together. "Go use the bathroom first. Then I'll drive you home."

"Okay." After one last, long look, she slides out of bed and disappears inside the bathroom.

Dropping back, I throw and arm over my head, squeeze my eyes shut and ignore my throbbing dick.

For some reason—a reason I'm trying not to think about too hard—I'm not quite ready to let go of Hannah Everson. And that's a damn dangerous thing for me.

After we both freshen up quickly, I escort her down to my car. She slides in and I shut the door, make my way around and get into the driver's side. Hannah gives me an address in Brooklyn and I plug it into the GPS. I'm not sure what I expect, but the closer we get to her place, the more my heart sinks. The neighborhood isn't great and I don't like what I'm seeing. I don't like it at all. The idea of her living in a dirty, crime-ridden neighborhood bothers me. A fucking lot.

"Right there," she says, pointing to a dumpy brick building.

Gritting my teeth, I pull up alongside the curb and turn the car off. "I'll walk you up."

"Are you sure? You don't have to—"

"I'm sure," I insist.

First, I want to check the place out and make sure everything is okay. Especially after she told me how Creed's man had broken in last night. We walk up to the front door and she opens it without using a key. Just pushes the damn thing open—which means anyone else could do the same.

"Why isn't there a lock?" I demand.

"Oh, there is. It's just, ah, broken. Maintenance keeps saying they'll fix it, but they're taking their good ol' time." She gives me a little shrug and I follow her, not liking that answer at all.

The inside isn't much better and I try not to cringe or judge. The carpet is old and worn, practically threadbare in places, and a musty smell hangs in the air. The dusty light fixture has two burned-out bulbs and I sneeze.

"Bless you," Hannah says as I automatically start toward the elevator. "Oh, ah, I usually take the stairs."

"Why?" I ask, almost not wanting to know the answer.

"I don't trust that elevator. It's gotten stuck one too many times. And, I'm only on the second floor, so it's not too bad."

This whole place is bad, I want to say, but I keep my mouth shut. *It's none of your business, Vin,* I tell myself. Don't worry about it.

Easier said than done, though. For whatever reason, Hannah is becoming my responsibility, a priority, and I want her to be safe and well taken care of.

Just like I figured, the front door to her apartment is still ajar and she immediately pauses. I walk past her and push the door all the way open. I scan the small living room area and adjacent kitchen. Nothing looks out of place. But, it's a sad, little place. With just a couch covered by a thin afghan and a worn-looking recliner, my frown deepens. A glance to the left shows me a miniscule kitchen that can barely fit a fridge and a very small table and two chairs.

Hannah Everson deserves so much better than this place. But what am I supposed to do about it?

"Wait here while I check the rest of the place out," I tell her and stride down the hallway. There's a small bathroom that you can barely turn around in and then one more doorway. I step through it and see it's her bedroom. A worn comforter covered in pink and green flowers covers the bed and I stalk forward and pull open the closet. It's nearly empty. A handful of hangers hold threadbare clothing and three pairs of shoes sit on the floor.

Shit. My chest tightens as it occurs to me that my angel has even less money than I realized. A part of me wants to immediately wire a million bucks into her account. Hell, I wouldn't even miss it. Besides, Enzo will make me that much money this year alone.

Running a hand along the top of a scarred dresser, I see it's missing a knob. I don't like Hannah living here. Not one fucking bit. *But what can I do to change that?* I wonder.

"Vin? Is everything okay?"

I turn and see her step into the room, a wary look on her beautiful face.

No, it's not okay, I want to tell her. *You're living in a shithole and you should be in a mansion.*

Instead, I turn to her and force a smile. "Yeah. The front door lock is broken, though. I'm going to send someone over to fix that right away, okay?"

"You don't have—"

AVA GRAY

"Consider it done," I interrupt, my voice gentle, but firm.

"Okay. Um, thanks."

She starts wringing her hands like she did before and I reach out and grab them, putting an end to the nervous gesture. "C'mon and walk me out."

Touching her feels so right, way too good, but I force myself to let go. *Later.* In the meantime, we walk back to the flimsy front door and I can't help but frown again. I stalk over to the tiny kitchen table, grab a chair and drag it over. "After I leave, wedge this under the doorknob. Don't open it again until the repairman comes, okay?"

"Okay."

After getting her phone number and programming it into my phone, I have to physically force myself to leave. "I'll be back at six o'clock," I remind her.

"We don't need to go anywhere fancy or anything," she says, looking a little nervous.

A flash of her limited wardrobe fills my head. "Don't worry about that. Wear whatever you're comfortable in and I'll see you soon."

"Thank you, Vin," Hannah says.

I nod then make myself turn and walk away. I have no idea why this is so damn hard, but everything inside of me wants to take her with me. Leaving her here doesn't sit well with me and I vow to change it.

How, though? I wonder again.

On the drive home, I call up one of the family security guards and tell him Hannah's address. I don't think Creed will cause any more problems but, just in case, I want someone stationed outside of Hannah's apartment to keep watch.

Getting her out of this neighborhood and that awful apartment is my first priority. Drumming my fingers against the steering wheel, I remember the new job I'm starting Monday and how I'm going to need an assistant.

Perfect.

I'll hire Hannah to be my executive assistant and pay her an outrageous salary so she can move into a better place. She said she didn't like her job at the diner and why would she? I can offer her something much better, stable, and, at the same time, I can keep a close eye on her. Keep her close to me.

Losing her mom was hard and the idea of her being all alone in this world guts me. Not anymore. From this point forward, Hannah has me. She may not know it yet, but I'm going to make sure my angel is taken care of. I have the means, so why the hell not? No woman has snagged my interest like this in so long. Which, of course, makes me nervous...it also makes me damn excited, too.

Take it easy, Vin, I warn myself. One step at a time. I'll see if she's interested in working at the wine company—why wouldn't she be?—and then we'll go from there. We'll have a nice dinner tonight and see how everything goes. I know she said she didn't want to go anywhere fancy, but screw that. I'm planning to wine and dine her like never before. I'm going to take her to the nicest restaurant in the city and feed her until she can't eat another bite. She's getting something better than a damn grilled cheese tonight. I plan to spoil her rotten. I can only imagine how hard her life has been lately with her mother passing and I want to take all of that pain and stress away.

I'm going to need some help, though, and I pull up Carlotta's number.

"Hi, Vin, what's up?" she answers.

"Hey, Lottie. I need a favor."

"Oh? What?"

I'm the self-sufficient brother, so I can hear the curiosity in her voice. "Keep this to yourself, please, but I need you to pick out a nice outfit.

Maybe a dress? And then have it sent to the address I give you."

"For who?"

I can hear the curiosity in her voice.

"A woman," I say, keeping it vague.

"Okaaaay. Obviously, duh. C'mon, give me more than that."

"No details yet, nosy."

"Well, I'm going to need to know a few things. Like where are you going, what size does she wear and what color is her hair?"

"Why do you need to know her hair color?" I ask suspiciously.

"Because..." Her voice trails off as she searches for a plausible answer. "So I can pick a color that will be flattering."

"Sure." Somehow, I don't quite believe her, but I tell her, anyway. "She has blonde hair, blue eyes and she's tiny. But curvy."

"Sounds like you've been busy, big brother," she teases. "She sounds pretty."

"She's more than pretty."

"Where did you meet?"

"I don't have time to get into details. Can you help me out or not?"

"You're lucky I have some free time and that you're my favorite brother."

I roll my eyes. She tells us all we're her favorite brother. I rattle off Hannah's name and address and my sister promises me she's on it.

"Thanks, Lottie. Put it on my tab and don't spare any expense."

"Oh, you bet I will. Are you sure you don't want me to hand-deliver the outfit myself? Because I can."

"No, nosy. Have a courier take care of it, please."

"Oh, alright."

"Thank you." I disconnect the call and shake my head. Carlotta is the baby and we all love her dearly, but she has to be the nosiest person I've ever met. She's always up in everyone's business and loves to gossip. I hope she doesn't decide to deliver the outfit she picks out, but there's no controlling my little sister. If she wants to do something then she'll do it no matter what we say.

A smile tugs at my mouth and I realize how damn much I'm looking forward to tonight and dinner with Hannah. Maybe if I'm really lucky, I'll get another kiss. If I'm supremely lucky, perhaps I'll be fortunate enough to share her bed again.

A man can dream, right?

7

HANNAH

I can't believe my savior asked me out to dinner tonight. My life has been on a downward spiral then hit rock bottom when my mom died. Then I broke through those rocks and plummeted down into a pile of shit when Dexter Creed sent his man after me and I was forced to participate in that awful auction last night. Somehow all of that washed away and when I looked off that stage into the crowd, I saw a pair of intense green eyes. Vin Rossi literally scooped me up into his arms and took me away from it all.

And now he wants to take me out to dinner.

I pinch myself and dance across the bedroom floor. Throwing my closet door open, my mood deflates a little. I have nothing to wear. What if he takes me to some fancy restaurant? I'm going to look like a poor relation. Oh, God, I don't want to embarrass myself. Or, worse, him. Sighing, I wonder how I'm going to find something nice to wear when there's a knock on my door.

Walking back into the living room, I ask who it is before removing the chair from beneath the door handle. It turns out to be the repairman Vin sent over. Wow, that was fast. But I have the impression that when Vin Rossi wants something done, it happens immediately. No one stops to ask any questions; they just carry out his orders.

Plucking the chair back, I open the door and smile at him. "Thank you for coming so soon."

He waves my words off.

"Not a problem, miss." I step back while he inspects the broken lock. "This shouldn't take me longer than ten minutes."

"Okay, thanks." While he starts getting his tools out, I notice a woman walking up the hallway and she lifts her sunglasses up onto her head as she approaches. She's strikingly gorgeous with long dark hair and big, brown eyes. I also notice how fashionable she looks and I wish I could pull off the kind of elegant confidence that she radiates.

"Hannah?" she asks, walking right up to my broken door, all glowy gorgeousness and what strikes me as curiosity.

"Uh, yeah." Who is this divine creature? I wish I was half as perfect.

"Hi, I have a special delivery for you from Vincentius Rossi." She whips the garment bag around she's carrying over her shoulder, along with another bag, and offers it to me.

"For me?" Suddenly, I'm so confused.

"For your date tonight," she clarifies.

I'm not sure what to say. Vin's kindness is overwhelming, but I take the proffered bag and smile at the woman. "Thank you so much. I can't believe he did this," I murmur under my breath more so to me than her.

"He's a very generous person," she tells me.

"Are you his, er, assistant?" I ask, not sure what to think about the beautiful woman. She looks a few years older than me and she's so well put together that it makes me feel frumpy.

She waves a perfectly-manicured hand through the air. "Oh, something like that. He is always wanting me to run his errands." Then she chuckles and tosses me a wink. "Have fun tonight."

I'm not sure what to think and I have no idea who she is, but I like her. Something about her is mysterious, yet kind, and I'll have to ask Vin later tonight. In the meantime, I can't stop thinking about my hero. There's no denying that I'm drawn to Vin. And I think it's more than just because he saved me from that other man.

Of course, I find him extremely attractive. What girl in her right mind wouldn't? But I'm also fascinated by him. Does he make it a habit of rescuing people like he did me? Or am I special? My cheeks heat up when I think about how much I owe him. Because I do. Vin paid a fortune for me and he didn't even try to claim his prize—which, in his defense, he could've done. He had every right to take my virginity last night. But he didn't even attempt it. All he did was place a quick kiss against my lips.

Our conversation comes back to me.

"Why did you spend so much money to buy me—er, my virginity—and you don't want to sleep with me?"

"I never said I don't want to sleep with you. But I won't take something that isn't freely given. And I've never paid for sex."

What was he doing at the White Auction then? He never really answered that. All I know is I'm the one who can't stop thinking about him and now I find myself wanting more. So much more.

The fact is I am a twenty-two year old virgin. Granted, that's not as old as some, but it's still older than most women when they sleep with a man for the first time. And, good God, Vin is all man. I can still remember how citrusy-delicious he smelled and how hard his chest felt against my hands. Yeah, there's no doubt about it—Vin Rossi is the perfect masculine specimen and he's got my pulse thundering, heart beating like crazy and, dare I say, my panties damp. Again.

Over the years, I haven't had time to date or explore a serious relationship with a man. Hence me still being a virgin at twenty-two. But now that my mom is gone and there's a drop-dead gorgeous man paying attention to me, things are shifting. I find myself experiencing things I haven't before. At least not to this degree. Desire is a new thing for me and it's making me all hot and bothered like I've never been before.

Chewing my lower lip, I set the bag with what I think are shoes down on the floor and hang the garment bag up and unzip it. I can't help but gasp when I look at the beautiful dress inside. Reaching out, I touch the dark red, silky fabric, running my fingers down its length. It's short and sexy. Wondering how Vin knew what size to send, I carefully take it off the hanger and check the tag. It's a six. How did he know my size?

Maybe he was checking me out more than I realized, I think with a little smile of satisfaction.

"All set!" a voice yells.

I snap out of my reverie and look over at the repairman who is now hefting his toolbox back up off the floor.

"Thank you so much," I tell him and hurry over.

"No problem."

"What do I owe you?"

But he shakes his head. "Nothing. Mr. Rossi has it covered."

"Oh, um, okay."

"Have a good day, miss."

"You, too." I wave and watch as he walks off. Then I close the door and test the new lock. It snaps shut and I feel a bit more secure than I did. I'm not used to someone taking care of me like this and, I'm not going to lie, it's really, really nice. Normally, I'm the caretaker and I'm the one who has to make sure everything is done and everyone is fine. But Vin is making sure I'm the one who's okay and it warms my heart.

The day flies by so fast and I spend most of it being nervous. I also spend a good portion of it getting ready. I take a long, luxurious shower and my thoughts turn wicked as I stand there under the falling water, running my hands over my wet, naked body and thinking about Vin. Imagining that my hands are his hands. Touching my breasts, sliding my hand between my thighs, I pretend he's in there with me. Pleasuring me.

Of course, it's not the same.

But I do come to a conclusion—I want to sleep with him tonight. Yes, I owe him, but it's so much more than that. Maybe I'm a little naive, but I trust him and I want him to be my first. Something tells me he's going to be a kind, gentle and considerate lover. Maybe even a little romantic. I want that, too. I want it all.

I want him.

I spend an inordinate amount of time dolling myself up with a little extra makeup and I make sure my hair is brushed until it shines like gold. Then I slip into the dress from Vin along with the sexy, strappy heels. Of course, they're my exact size, and I do a little spin in front of the mirror. I don't think I've ever felt so beautiful. Almost like Cinderella.

Promptly at six o'clock, there's a knock on my door and my stomach drops. *Oh, God, he's here.* Forcing myself to pull in a deep, steadying breath, I smooth my clammy hands down the front of my dress, walk over and open the door.

Standing before me is the god of all gods. My heart skips up my throat and I can't believe this beautiful man is here to pick me up and take me out to dinner. Who am I? How did my luck turn around in the past twenty-four hours to the point that I'm practically giddy? Maybe I'm dreaming.

Vin's gaze slides down me and I nearly swoon. He looks amazing in a perfectly-tailored, charcoal-colored suit but, like last night, he's not wearing a tie. When those panther-like green eyes lift back up and meet mine, I give him a shy smile.

"Hi," I say softly.

"Hi," he answers. "You look stunning."

A fierce blush steals over my cheeks. "Thank you. The dress and shoes fit perfectly. You didn't have to—"

"I wanted to," he interrupts me. "And you look amazing in that color."

I must look like a fool because I'm grinning so damn hard. "You did a good job. Or, your assistant did," I correct myself.

"Assistant?" he echoes, frowning slightly.

"Oh, the woman who dropped them off with the long dark hair. She was really nice."

A funny look passes over his handsome face and then his mouth edges up. "Did my 'assistant' happen to introduce herself?" he asks, voice dry.

I shake my head.

"I'm guessing you met my sister, Carlotta. I asked her to pick out the dress and shoes for you tonight."

Sister? I wasn't expecting that. "Oh! She was lovely."

"I'm sure."

I can't help but chuckle at his sarcastic tone. A wave of relief also passes through me now that I know they're related because she is the exact kind of woman I imagine Vin would be attracted to and date. Not me.

"C'mon," he says. "I hope you're hungry because I'm taking you to the best Italian restaurant in the city."

69

"Starving," I say and he glances down at me. There's no mistaking the heat in his emerald eyes and I swallow hard, trying to ignore my nerves.

Vin clears his throat and we head down to his car. It's the same Mercedes I rode in before and I slide in, settling on the soft, buttery leather seat. Suddenly, I feel so very much like my fairytale is coming true. No one has ever spoiled me like this before and it's nice. But I don't want to get used to it. As far as Vin and I are concerned...well, I'm going to offer him myself tonight, but I don't expect anything more than one night. We're clearly from two different worlds and I don't belong in his. However, for the time being, it's going to be really nice to visit. I'm harboring no illusions, though, and I'll be ready when the Mercedes turns back into a pumpkin.

Vin pulls the car right up to the valet and my door instantly opens. A young man helps me out as Vin circles around. I could swear, he sends a glare at the valet before tossing his key fob over and possessively placing a hand on my back and steering me away.

We walk up the stairs and pause at the podium where the hostess recognizes Vin right away.

"Hello, Mr. Rossi. Your table is ready. Please, follow me."

Wow. Talk about a reception. As we walk through the restaurant, skirting other tables and diners, I look around and I'm beyond impressed. Candles flicker on each tabletop and large crystal chandeliers emit a low light giving the whole place a very romantic atmosphere. Soft music plays from hidden speakers and the smell of the food is delicious.

Vin keeps his hand firmly on my back as the hostess escorts us over to a private, corner table. A candle flickers in its center and the silverware practically sparkles. After pushing my chair in, Vin sits down across from me, studying me in the dim lighting.

"What?" I ask softly, feeling self-conscious.

70

"Nothing. Just admiring how beautiful you look tonight."

Blushing again, I look down and start fussing with the edge of a knife. "Oh, um, thank you. You look very nice, too."

"Hannah?"

"Hmm?" I look back up and see the desire flare to life in his green eyes.

"I'm serious. When you first opened your door, you took my breath away."

Oh, my God. What do I even say to that? I clasp my hands together and try to wrangle my nerves. Before I can respond, a short, slightly over-weight man with a big smile and friendly eyes walks over and shakes hands with Vin.

"Good evening," he greets us warmly. "It's so nice to see you again."

"You, too. Mario, I'd like you to meet Hannah," Vin says. "Hannah, this is Mario Agresti, the owner."

"It's so nice to meet you," I say and we shake hands.

"The pleasure is all mine."

He and Vin talk for a minute and then food starts arriving at the table before we even order. A waiter pours a glass of red wine for each of us and my eyes must go wide as saucers because Vin and Mario chuckle.

"Only the best service for my dear friends," Mario says. "I hope you enjoy the sampling and, of course, the wine from Rossi Vineyard."

We thank him and then I look at all the plates of food, not sure where to start. Once again, Vin steps in and serves me then himself. He explains each dish as we make our way through them all and by the time we've tasted everything, I have my favorites. I've also finished a glass of wine and I'm feeling lighter than I have in years.

Licking my lips, I look across the table and smile at Vin. My Prince Charming is going to be well-rewarded tonight for treating me with such kindness and respect. I'm going to repay him with my virginity and I look forward to spending the night in his arms.

He just doesn't know it yet.

8

VIN

Watching Hannah eat, drink and delight everyone around her makes me happy. Happier than I've been in a very long time. She's artless, sincere and gorgeous as hell. I think the most attractive thing to me is that she doesn't even know how amazing she truly is.

When I think back over my time with Cynda, it never felt like this. Not even in the beginning when things were new and fresh. Cynda always had this worldly air and she was quite aware of her beauty. She wielded it with a cool power to get whatever and whoever she wanted. I didn't recognize it at first, but she used me, too. Unfortunately, I caught on to her deception too late.

Hannah, on the other hand, is a much-needed breath of fresh air. She's a goddamn delight. We talk over our meal and the conversation never lags. She's witty and smart. Maybe refreshing is the best adjective to describe her. The total opposite of Cynda who turned out to be conniving and deceitful. I learned my lesson, though. The hard way. I'm not stupid enough to ever give my heart to another woman again, but Hannah tempts that notion sorely. She makes me want things that

I've made off-limits. Hannah Everson is a temptation that I wasn't expecting, but I'm enjoying every moment with her thoroughly.

After we finish eating far too much food, Mario's wonderful staff removes the dishes and brings out an array of desserts. It's all way too much, but it all looks so good. Utterly decadent and I pick up my fork.

"Ready for some dessert?" I ask Hannah and she places a hand over her stomach.

"I feel like I'm going to explode. I don't think I've ever eaten so much in my life."

Her admission makes me grin. Hell, anything she says has been bringing a smile to my face all evening. "Let's just take a taste," I say and reach for the plate of cannoli. Sliding my fork through the flaky pastry shell, I scoop up some of the creamy, sweet ricotta filling. "Cannoli is a staple Sicilian dessert. We can't not eat it. That would be a shame."

She laughs and I lift my fork, lean forward and offer her the first bite. Without hesitation, Hannah presses closer and wraps her mouth around my fork, pulling the bite of sweetness right off the edge. I watch her chew then lick her lips, and my dick is about to tear through my pants at the sight. She's so damn lovely it's sinful. And, God knows, the things I want to do to this woman are downright wicked and, possibly, slightly sinful.

Willing the throbbing in my pants to go away, or at least to settle down, I send her a smile. "Well? What do you think of Agresti's cannoli?"

"Ohmygod," she breathes, pressing her full lips together, "it's so good."

Forcing myself to look away before I blow and thoroughly embarrass myself, I sweep another bite of cannoli onto my fork and eat it. Yeah, it's delicious. But, not even half as good as I imagine the beauty sitting across from me would taste. All I can think about is pulling that little red dress up, sliding her panties to the side and licking her sweet, wet pussy. Just thinking about the way she moaned as she ate the cannoli off my fork makes me grit my teeth and will my unruly dick to go down. But, I can't help but wonder how that moan would sound right before she screams my name as I'm riding her hard.

Fuck. I swipe a hand over my face and try to shut down the lust currently setting my blood on fire. But, it's getting harder and harder not to picture her naked and writhing beneath me. I know she would take me so well, take all of me so deep. And she'd be so wet, dripping for me. Only me.

She's a virgin, asshole. The last thing on my mind should be bedding Hannah. Especially after what she went through last night. I can only imagine how much it might've traumatized her. Not being able to choose the first man you sleep with and being threatened with rape in order to pay off your debt must've been terrifying for her. My poor, precious angel. The last thing I want is for her to be scared of sex. That would be a goddamn tragedy. With that luscious body of hers, I have no doubt that she has the potential to be an absolute sexual goddess between the sheets.

And, God help me, I want a taste. I want to know what it feels like to slide into her hot pussy. I want to experience the moment of her first release with a man and know how it feels to have her slick core clench around my stiff cock and milk me hard. Maybe I'm being a selfish bastard, but I can't help it. It's been a long time since lust has had such a fierce grip on me and I'm not sure how to handle it.

This isn't the wine talking either. I'm completely sober and only allowed myself one glass. The rest of the time I drank water. I've also counted how many glasses of wine Hannah has drunk—two. So, yeah, she's definitely feeling good. But she's not stumbling-down drunk or anything. She seems giddy and happily buzzing, but still able to make an informed decision. She's able to give consent if things go that way. And, God help me, I want them to go that way. I want it so damn badly, I ache.

As wonderful as dinner is, eventually it's time to go. I leave Mario and his staff an outrageous tip then stand up, walk over and pull Hannah's chair out. I watch her get up, gauging how steady she is on her feet, especially wearing those sexy heels, and she appears perfectly stable. Thank Christ. Otherwise, I'd be a real letch for what I'm thinking about doing.

"Okay?" I ask and reach for her elbow.

"I'm good," she assures me, grasping onto my arm.

I love the feel of her holding onto me and I guide her through the dining area. After a quick thank-you to Mario, I take Hannah outside and we wait for the valet to bring my car around. She's leaning against me and I look down as she looks up.

"You're so pretty," she whispers and I burst out laughing.

"How drunk are you, Hannah?' I ask. Because as much as I want to be with her, I won't do anything but take her home if she's not in the right state of mind.

She thinks over my question then smiles. "I've had enough wine to feel good, but not too much that I want to pass out."

"That's reassuring," I mumble. I'm still not sure and I'm starting to wonder if I should just take her back to her place. The longer I keep her around, the way she's touching me, the way my nose is filling with her baby powder scent, it's making it harder and harder not to jump her.

"Vin?"

"Yes?"

"Can I go home with you?"

My heart kicks hard against my ribs and I'm speechless for a moment. "Angel," I finally say, brushing a hand over her blonde hair, "you can have whatever you want."

"Can I have you?" she asks, not missing a beat.

"Me?" I need to be completely clear with her request. "What exactly do you want, sweet girl?"

"I want to pay you back for being so kind to me."

"You don't owe me a damn thing, do you understand?" I need her to know I have no expectations.

"Yes. Thank you."

"You're welcome."

We're still staring at each other when the valet pulls my Mercedes up to the curb. I help Hannah inside, tip the guy and then get in on the driver's side. An internal debate is going on in my head. Do I take Hannah home or—

"I want to go to your place," she says, voice firm.

My fingers grip the steering wheel hard. "Hannah, I need you to know that if you come home with me...I'm going to want things...I'm going to want *you*. You're tempting me sorely and I'm not going to be able to hold myself back."

"Good. Because I want you, too," she informs me in a breathy voice.

My foot hits the gas pedal hard and, as we screech forward, Hannah bursts into laughter. I reach over and grab her hand, squeezing it hard. *My angel.* The thought comes out of nowhere and I want her to be mine. In every way possible.

"If you let me, I'm going to give you the best night of your life." There's no ego in my words, just the absolute truth. I will worship this woman. She tightens her grip on my hand.

"I hope so," she whispers, and I'm a goner.

I can't get us back to my place fast enough. The moment we step into the elevator, my patience disappears in a puff. I yank Hannah into my arms and my mouth crashes down against hers. Her arms wrap around my neck, her perfect breasts crushing against my chest, and I groan into her mouth. She feels so damn good against me, her body molding along mine perfectly. The moment her lips part, I slide my tongue inside her mouth and caress it against hers. God, she tastes like sweet cream and absolute decadence.

We kiss and kiss and kiss until the cab reaches my floor. The elevator door glides open and we stumble out, our mouths still fused. I'm fumbling for my keys and when we reach my door, I pull back, breathing hard. She grips onto me to keep from falling over and seems just as affected by that steamy kiss as I was. Shoving the key into the lock, I open the door, pull Hannah inside then slam it shut, locking it. I grab her and haul her right back into my arms. She instantly surrenders to my kiss, melting against me.

For a long time, we stand there in the foyer, kissing each other sense-less. My hands slide through her blonde hair, tilting her head so I can deepen the connection between our mouths. I can't seem to get enough and when she makes a soft whimpering sound, I nearly lose it.

Forcing myself to step back, I swipe a hand through my hair. I've never wanted a woman this much before and I'm feeling a little off-balance. And it's got nothing to do with the glass of wine I drank.

Hannah stands before me, a tempting sight in that red dress. Her skin is flushed, cheeks pink and lips swollen from my heated kisses.

"I need to taste you again," I say, my voice hoarse.

"Then kiss me," she whispers huskily.

I hold out my hand and she doesn't hesitate to take it. "I plan on kissing you somewhere else this time," I say and tug her toward my bedroom.

"Oh!" she gasps, jogging to keep up with my long strides. "And where may I ask do you plan on kissing me next?" Her teasing voice makes the steel beam in my pants extend even further.

78

We reach my bedroom and I spin her around, my hands grabbing her hips, and I pull her up against me, making her aware of how much I want her. I grind my hips against her pelvis, knowing she can feel how fucking hard I am.

"Right between these lovely legs," I answer, my hands dipping beneath her dress and sliding up her silky thighs.

"Ohhh," she responds breathlessly.

"Is that okay?" I start nibbling the side of her neck, flicking my tongue across the delicate skin there.

"Yes..." She sighs softly. "It's more than okay."

That's all the encouragement I need. Sliding my hands under her ass, I scoop her up and her legs instantly wrap around my waist. She weighs practically nothing and I move over to the bed and lay her out. Flipping her skirt up, my gaze drops to soak in her light pink panties and I stifle a groan. She's too beautiful, too innocent. It's making me crazy and my desire is at an all-time high, ready to consume me like I'm about to consume her. Meanwhile, my dick is at full attention and weeping to get between those luscious legs. Not yet, though. First, I'm going to taste that sweet pussy, coat my lips and tongue with her nectar. I'm going to show her what it feels like to have my head between her thighs, eating her out until she's screaming for more.

Propped up on her elbows, she's looking at me and I can see the innocence shining in her bright blue eyes. I'm going to claim that innocence, take it as mine, and cherish it. She's giving me a gift and I'll make damn sure she doesn't regret that decision.

Time to reward my angel with multiple orgasms, I think, as I hook my fingers in her panties and begin to slowly slide them down.

9

HANNAH

My breath catches in my throat as Vin slides my panties down, baring me to him. I'm not sure what to do and I automatically try to squeeze my legs together, but he grabs hold of my thighs, stopping me. Slowly pulling them apart, exposing my most intimate place.

"No," he murmurs, green eyes blazing as he gazes down on me. "Open your legs, Angel. Let me taste you."

Heart in my throat, I do as he says, and when he lowers his head, his mouth latching onto my center, I whimper softly. I've never experienced anything like this before and his tongue laps and licks and strokes until I'm writhing. My fingers dig into the bedspread and a pressure begins building in my lower body. The moment he begins sucking on my clit, I lose it. A zap of electricity shoots through me and everything suddenly explodes in waves of pleasure. I cry out and twist as the orgasm rocks through me.

Breathing hard, eyes squeezed tightly shut, I wonder if I've been missing out or if it's Vin who is the reason I feel so amazing right now. He crawls up my body and whispers, "Open your eyes, Angel."

My lashes flutter open and I look into his intense green eyes. He reminds me of a very satisfied panther and then his mouth crashes against mine. As he kisses me passionately, I lose all control and wrap my arms around him. Pushing up off the mattress, I press my body against his and a wave of need moves through me. Tasting myself on his mouth is strangely erotic and I drag my tongue over his bottom lip, licking.

"See how good you taste. Like sugar."

I moan softly when his hand moves down and begins stroking between my legs. He knows exactly what he's doing because it doesn't take long before I'm pushing against his palm, searching for that release. He slides a finger inside me and I shamelessly move as he thrusts it in and out.

"Christ, you're tight. And so wet."

Vin adds a second finger, stretching me, and I arch up. The pleasure is building all over again and his thumb finds my clit, pressing down, as his fingers fill and scissor, stretching me even further. He doesn't have small fingers either. They're long and so much bigger than mine. And, clearly, they're built to make a woman feel so freaking good.

I cry out, my inner muscles contracting, and fall back against the bed. A dazed feeling comes over me as my second orgasm passes. *God, he's good at this,* I think. I'm so damn glad I waited because giving Vin my virginity has been the best decision I might've ever made. Maybe even the highlight of my life so far. And it isn't even over yet.

He lifts his weight up off the mattress and I watch with heavy lids as he slowly unbuttons his shirt. I could be wrong, but it looks like his fingers are trembling slightly. They're also slick with my wetness and I can't help but flush. He tosses the shirt, unbuckles his belt then chucks it along with his trousers. My nerves kick up a notch when I look down and see his tented boxer briefs. Oh, boy, he's huge. Even bigger than I had imagined. Chewing on my lower lip, it occurs to me that his fingers had barely fit inside me. How in the world am I going to manage his cock?

Before I can think too hard about it, he pulls me forward and slips the dress over my head. My bra's clasp unsnaps and he pulls it slowly down my arms, his green eyes darkening a shade as he gazes at my bare breasts. Feeling self-conscious, I try to cover myself, but he grabs my wrists.

"Don't. You're far too beautiful to hide." Vin lifts my arms above my head and rasps, "Lay down."

I fall back on the bed and he holds my wrists down, pinned against the mattress, then dips his head and begins worshiping my breasts. It's the best word I can use to describe what he's doing. He takes his time, slowly licking and caressing with his tongue. Pulling first one nipple then the other into his mouth and sucking.

"Oh, God," I moan. It feels so good. He feels so good. I'm obscenely wet, arching against his mouth, and as nervous as I am about his size, I'm aching for more. I'm aching for him to be inside of me. To possess me completely. "Vin, I need you."

"Are you ready?" he asks huskily, reaching down and sliding a finger inside me again.

"Yes," I rasp.

"So ready," he purrs, kissing me again. He spread my wetness up and around my clit and I cry out.

Then he pulls away and I open my eyes, feeling the loss immediately. "Vin…"

"Patience, Angel." He pushes up, drags the nightstand drawer open and pulls out a small silver packet. Then he shoves his boxer briefs off and I press my lips together, watching as he rips the package open and rolls the condom down his pulsating length.

My hand reaches for him and I wrap my fingers around him. My fingers don't even touch, unable to fully circle his girth. "Umm..." I swallow hard. "You're really big."

"You can take me," he assures me and settles himself between my thighs. "I know you can, Angel."

I hope I can. They say your first time hurts and it's been so good up until now. But I'm determined to do this. To give Vin as much pleasure as he's given me.

"Relax and open up to me," he encourages, pressing his thick tip against my center. Parting my folds, he slides in slightly and I gasp. "I'll go slowly."

He can go as slowly as he wants, but that doesn't make his cock any smaller or hurt any less. But when his fingers find my clit and start working their magic again, everything in me relaxes. My thighs fall completely open and I hook my ankles around his legs. He's being so gentle, and I can tell it's killing him to go this slow. His muscles are straining and his jaw is tight, teeth gritted. I can feel my body stretching as he slides in a little further, but mostly I feel another orgasm coming on. The moment it hits, I cry out and that's when Vin thrusts home.

The sting is brief and takes a moment to fade. I look up and he's staring at me, hips pumping, filling me with his cock. I've never experienced a physical connection like this with another person and all I can do is hold on tightly.

"You feel so good," he rasps. "Like heaven."

It doesn't take me long to realize that Vin is the consummate lover. When it's time to be gentle he is and when it's time to increase the friction and make me scream, he delivers. Oh, my God, does he deliver in spades.

"Vin!" He's moving faster—cock and fingers—and it's all too much. The way we're connected, how deeply he's penetrating me, body and soul, and the delicious taste of his kiss, so deep and thorough, is all too much. He's driving me straight to the edge and I hover there, shaking and on the verge of tumbling over.

"Come for me, Angel. Come on my cock," he urges.

His dirty words are all it takes to send me flying over the edge and spiraling into another orgasm of epic proportion. I cry out and bite down on his shoulder making him grunt. He continues thrusting then blows with a growled curse. Burying my face in his shoulder, I feel him go stiff and shudder.

For a long moment, he stays inside me and we lay there, breathing hard. When he finally pulls out and rolls off me, I feel an immediate loss. I like the warm heaviness of his body on mine. Turning my head, I see his chest rising and falling hard, and he's lying on his back, staring up at the ceiling. He looks almost as dazed as I am which surprises me. While this is all new to me, I know it certainly isn't for him.

Right?

I can't help but wonder if he felt some of the connection that I did? Did he think what just happened was amazing, too? God, I hope so.

When he finally turns and looks over at me, I can't read him. His green eyes are shielded and worry spikes up within me. But then he presses a soft kiss to my shoulder and slips out of bed. As he walks to the attached bathroom, I can't help but admire his broad back, tight ass and long legs. His body is ridiculously beautiful. I've never admired a man's body before, but Vin's deserves to be worshiped in every possible way.

I have no idea what to expect now. Is he going to kick me out? Send me home? Or pull me into his arms and hold me? Maybe I should get up and put my dress back on. He's taking longer than I expected to get rid of the protection and my nerves are escalating. I don't know the proper etiquette post-sex and I chew on my lower lip, debating whether or not I should make a run for it.

As I sit up and grab the sheet to cover myself, he reappears and he has a washcloth in his hand.

"Lay back," he murmurs, sitting down on the bed.

I hesitate and he tugs the sheet down, baring me to him. I know I shouldn't be embarrassed after everything that we just did, but my cheeks flame when he begins to gently clean me. Glancing down, I see the blood on my thighs and his sheets. *Shit.* "I'm sorry," I whisper as humiliation consumes me.

"Sorry?" he echoes and pauses in his ministrations. "What the hell for?"

"Um, I'll wash your sheets…" God, this is awkward. Suddenly, I want to grab my clothes and bolt.

"No, you won't," he murmurs and starts cleaning me again. His eyes lock with mine. "You're mine, Hannah. And your blood on my cock and sheets is proof."

There's a possessive edge in his tone that surprises me. But I like it. A lot. I want to be his, in every possible way, but I'm sure he just means right now, at this very moment. Me, though? I'm thinking more long-term.

I'm not sure how to respond to that, so I don't. Vin gets rid of the washcloth then climbs back into bed beside me. I'm still debating whether or not I should leave when he reaches over and pulls me into his arms. A wave of relief passes through me.

He wants mme here.

Vin presses a kiss in my hair, encouraging me to lay my cheek on his chest. His arms hold me close as he whispers, "Go to sleep, Angel."

And that's exactly what I do. Surrounded by his warmth once again, I drift off into a peaceful slumber.

I can feel the warm sun hitting my bare legs and I roll onto my back and open my eyes. Everything that happened last night comes careening back through my brain and I realize Vin isn't in bed with me. I let my hand drift over where he was lying and it's cool to the touch. Sitting up, I wonder where he is and how long he's been gone.

As if in answer, he suddenly appears, striding into the bedroom, already showered and dressed in a suit. Minus a tie, of course. "Good morning," he says.

His tone is a little brisk and I'm not sure what to make of it.

"Good morning," I say, quickly turning shy, and pulling the sheet up to my chin.

Vin drops down on the edge of the bed and eyes me closely. "How're you feeling?"

"I'm okay." Truthfully, I'm sore, but I don't want to tell him that.

He nods. "Good. I have some work to do today. Whenever you're ready, I can drop you off at home."

His cool words take me by complete surprise. "Sure," I murmur, hating his brusque tone. *It's official—he's kicking me out.* I'm not sure what I expected exactly, but it wasn't this. Maybe breakfast in bed? A shower together? More sex? I would've loved to have spent the day together or...I don't know...something.

Instead, I'm getting a ride home. I guess it's better than him kicking me to the curb and expecting me to catch the bus. God, that would be the worst ride of shame ever.

At what point did he turn cool? What did I miss? Did I do something? Or, is this it? He got what he wanted and now it's over?

Over before it even began, I think sadly.

"I have a proposition for you," he says, adjusting the cuffs of his shirt beneath the suit jacket.

Oh? He just snagged my attention and I lean closer, cocking an eyebrow.

"As you know, I'm going to be heading the Rossi Vineyard division. I'll need an assistant and I'd like to offer you the job."

I stare at him blankly, not sure what to say or how to react. Why would he want me as his assistant? I have no office experience. Is it out of guilt? For taking my virginity? Because he knows I don't have much money? Or is it because he actually likes me and wants to see me again?

"Okaaay," I say slowly.

His dark, thick brows furrow. "Okay what?"

"I'll think about it."

That handsome face of his screws up into a deep scowl. "Think about what?"

"About whether or not to take the job as your assistant," I say carefully. He looks a little stunned and, at the same time, annoyed.

"What's there to think about?"

"Well, what would be my hours, what are your expectations and we haven't even discussed salary."

"Your hours would be for as long as I need you. My expectations are that you do a good job. And your salary will start at one-hundred thousand dollars a year including benefits and three weeks of paid vacation."

I blink, unable to comprehend that many zeroes. He mistakes my silence and instantly ups the offer.

"Okay, one twenty-five."

"Um…" I'm at a loss. That's more money that I can even understand, much less ever dream that I would make.

"One-forty."

"Stop!" I hold up my hand, feeling dizzy.

His green, guarded eyes narrow. "Is there a problem?"

"No, it's just this is happening really fast and I…I'd like to think it over. Please."

A muscle flexes in his cheek and he's about to say something more, but then clamps his jaw tight. "Fine," he finally grits out, not looking pleased at all. "But I'm not sure what the hell you need to think about."

He grumbles the last part under his breath and I'm about to reply when his gaze drops, heating up fast. The sheet slipped and I look down to see I'm giving him a pretty good view of the tops of my breasts. A part of me wants to let it go completely and see what he'll do. Instead, I'm too chicken and I pull it back up.

Vin clears his throat then pushes up off the bed. "I'll be waiting in the kitchen."

His tone is cool and my heart breaks a little. I'm not sure what I did and I wish I had someone to talk to because I really need a friend right now.

The drive back to my apartment isn't much better. It's clear Vin's walls are up and they're damn solid. But if he wanted to get rid of me, why would he ask me to work for him? I don't think I've ever been so confused in my life.

The ride to my place is quiet and I'm so deep in thought. Eventually, Vin pulls the Mercedes up to the curb in front of my building and then turns to face me. I'm already reaching for the door handle, ready to run, when he grabs my arm.

"Hannah…"

My eyes meet his and that blank stare he gave me earlier is now a swirling green storm of emotions. I don't say anything, just wait for him to continue.

"Last night was amazing. Sorry if I'm acting cool." He runs his hand down my arm in a soft caress, takes my hand in his and squeezes. "I'm just...anxious about this new position that I'm starting."

His excuse sounds lame, even to my ears. But, I nod, trying not to let him see how hurt my feelings really are.

"I want you to work for me. I'll call you tonight, okay?"

"Okay," I whisper. He releases my hand and I open the door and slip out, more confused than ever. Turning, I watch him drive away.

He didn't even kiss me goodbye.

My heart hurts as I push the still-broken front door open, walk upstairs and go into my quiet, very lonely and extremely empty apartment. I feel so lost, so confused. Heart heavy, I change out of my dress and carefully hang it in my closet. I slip on a pair of leggings and a t-shirt. Then I pull on a light sweatshirt and my tennis shoes.

Swiping my keys back up, I leave my apartment again and go to ask my mom for advice.

The cemetery is quiet, just a few birds singing above me in the trees when I sit down in front of her grave. I tuck my legs beneath me and run my hand over the cool gravestone. "I miss you, Mom," I whisper.

Maybe, just maybe, there's some way she can hear me. I hope so, anyway, because I don't think I've ever been so confused or desperate for advice.

"I met someone," I say softly. "His name is Vin—Vincentius, actually. What a name, right? He's Italian and so very handsome. Well, I was in some trouble and he swept in and saved me from some really bad men. He bought me a pretty dress and took me to dinner. No one's ever treated me so kindly. I could fall so easily for him." My voice catches. *Oh, God.* How can I develop feelings for someone so quickly? Is it possible? The ache in my heart tells me it is.

"But, this morning, he suddenly turned cool and now I have no idea what that means or how to handle it. Especially since he wants me to come work for him."

I pluck a piece of vibrant green grass from the ground and immediately see Vin's stunning green eyes.

"I don't know what to do, Mom. The more time I spend with him, the more it's going to hurt if he doesn't want me the way I want him. But I'd be foolish not to take the job. You know how much I hate working at the diner and being on my poor feet all day. This would allow me to sit at a desk and use my brain. I know I could do it—and do it really well. Plus, he's offering me an obscene amount of money and all the perks."

As much as I wanted to accept his offer right away, I didn't because of the way he suddenly turned cool. Everything had been going so well and then I could literally feel him pulling away and becoming guarded. I don't understand why and it hurts my feelings. I've never been in a situation like this before and I don't want to make the wrong decision.

I also don't want to get hurt further. Because Vincentius Rossi has the power to break my heart.

I let out a soft sigh and look up at the blue sky above. Even though she isn't here with me physically any longer, I know in my heart of hearts that my mom is listening. As I'm debating what I'm going to do, a bright red cardinal lands on the tombstone beside me. My jaw drops and tears sting my eyes. Cardinals represent loved ones visiting you after they've passed and my heart swells.

"I love you, Mom," I whisper. The beautiful bird looks at me for a moment and I feel an indescribable peace settle over me.

And I know what I'm going to do. I'm going to accept Vin's job offer.

Letting out a breath, I watch the cardinal fly away then stand up. Brushing my pants off, I walk back through the cemetery and out the main gates.

Out of nowhere, a prickling sensation touches the back of my neck. It feels like someone is watching me and I look around, but don't see anyone suspicious or anything at all unusual. Brushing it off, I continue heading up the sidewalk when a car pulls up to the curb.

"Well, hello," a masculine voice says and I pause and glance over.

I instantly recognize the man from the auction. The one who tried to buy me but, thankfully, Vin outbid him.

"You might not remember me—"

"I remember you," I say coolly.

"Well, I'm sorry things didn't turn out as I'd hoped. I wanted to get to know you better the other night."

I'm sure.

"I'm Caleb Durant." He looks at me, as though waiting for some kind of reaction. I don't know if he expects me to recognize his name, but I have no idea who he is. Nor do I care. He's still just as slimy as I remember.

"I really have to go," I say and start walking again.

"Mary! Wait! Can I give you a ride?"

I pause mid-step and bite my lip. I don't intend to tell him my true name or get in his fancy BMW. "I'm fine, thanks."

"Aww, don't be like that. C'mon, get inside and I'll drive you wherever you want to go."

"No, thank you." My voice is crisp and my dislike of him should be quite clear.

His dark eyes narrow and I can tell he's not happy with my answer. He's probably a man who's used to getting his way. *Oh, well. Not today.*

"Alright then," he relents, clearly unhappy. "Maybe another time."

"I don't think so." The last thing I want to do is encourage him. I have no interest.

"We'll see about that," he mutters then squeals away from the curb.

"What a jerk," I grumble. *No, Caleb Durant, you can be sure that I will not change my mind. Not about you. Not ever.*

10

VIN

T houghts of Hannah fill my head, teasing and tormenting me for hours after I dropped her off back home. I'm pissed at myself because I said I had to work, but I'm not working today. I don't officially start until Monday, but I needed some space from the bewitching beauty who is making me think all sorts of things I'm not used to thinking. She's making me want things. Impossible things.

So, I did the only thing I could—I went into self-preservation mode and got her out of here before I did something I would later regret.

Now I'm wishing I would've kept her here and that we were back in my bed. Because, goddamn it, Hannah Everson rocked my world last night. I woke up every hour and wanted to start kissing and touching her again. But, I didn't. I held myself back, fought my desire, knowing that she was probably sore and tired. Then I forced myself to let her go, slid out of bed and went out on the balcony to try and clear my head.

It didn't work. A shower didn't help either. Nor did getting dressed and drinking coffee. At some point last night, I not only fucked

Hannah, I fucked myself. Because as much as I want to deny and ignore it, I care about her. My angel is sweet, innocent and kind. She's exactly what I've always wanted in a partner, but that's what scares the hell out of me. Hannah is all the things that my ex wasn't, but I refuse to open my heart again. It's not worth the inevitable pain that always happens because relationships never last. No matter how badly you want them to. I learned my lesson the hard way—but I did learn it and I refuse to be one of those fools who repeats a mistake.

Fool me once, shame on you. Fool me twice, shame on me.

Even though I'm keeping my walls up and heart guarded, maybe we can still be physical. Sure, my emotions will be kept in check and locked down tight, but maybe she'd want to have a physical relationship. I know she deserves more, but I simply can't give it to her. I can, however, give us both more pleasure and make sure she has a body and bed to keep her warm.

Dammit, I know I'm walking a slippery slope and I need to be careful or I could fall for her. It would be so easy to do, too. Spending the day with Hannah wasn't an option. Not when I'm trying to keep my distance from the tempting beauty.

So, like a stubborn fool, I spend the day all alone in my big apartment and torture myself with thoughts of Hannah and how amazing it felt when I was deep inside her sweet, wet heat. At some point, I growl in frustration and grab my phone. I'm really fucking confused and need some advice. Since Enzo already knows about the auction, I call him. Enzo suggests we meet at the bar for a drink and he wants to hear all about the auction and what happened.

It doesn't take me long to reach Maximilian's, an upscale place where businessmen like my brother Enzo hang out. I think Enzo will help me figure out the situation. He may be a little younger than me, but he's a level-headed businessman. He's also a charmer who never lacks women. Enzo understands the danger of being a billionaire mafia son and what it means when everyone looks at you with his or her hand out.

I spot Enzo at a corner table, nursing a whiskey, and I walk over and sit down across from him.

"Hey, big brother," he says in greeting. "What's got your panties in a bunch?"

Enzo can read me only too well. "How about that fucking sex auction you sent me to the other night?"

He instantly sobers. "I'm sorry, Vin. I had no idea it was like that. I just thought you might be able to go and pick up somebody. I didn't realize you had to pay for it."

"One-hundred fifty six thousand dollars, to be exact," I murmur under my breath and motion to the waiter to bring me a whiskey like my brother's.

Vin chokes. "*What?* Jesus. That pussy better be sparkling with diamonds and come with a 401K for that amount of money."

I hesitate. He doesn't realize yet that I actually bid on someone. But, again, Enzo can read people extremely well and his dark eyes go wide.

"Wait. Are you saying that *you* bought someone?" he asks incredulously, his dark eyes going comically wide.

"I bid on her and won, yeah."

"Holy fucking shit." A huge grin fills his face. "Never in a million years would I have pictured you paying for sex."

"We didn't have sex." I hesitate, thinking over what happened. "Well, not that night."

"Oh, my God, Vin, what the hell have I missed in the last two days?"

I nod my thanks as the waiter places a glass of whiskey in front of me. God knows, I need some alcohol before I launch into this clusterfuck of a story. After a long, satisfying sip, I focus on my brother. "I was about to leave the auction when a woman walked onto the stage and I knew something wasn't right. She looked terrified and a couple of creeps started bidding on her. So, I outbid them and got her out of there."

"Such a hero." My brother grins from ear to ear.

"Shut up, Enzo. If it weren't for you, I wouldn't even be in this mess."

"How's it a mess? Sounds like you got yourself a woman."

I suppose he's right, but falling for Hannah is a huge problem. "Her name is Hannah. Dexter Creed, the loan shark, was forcing her to auction her virginity off to pay her debt back to him."

My brother's face screws up in distaste. "Fucker," he grumbles.

"Yeah, big-time fucker."

"Sorry, bro. I swear I didn't know it was that kind of auction."

I shrug a shoulder. "I got her out of there and we spent the night together, but nothing happened. Not until last night, anyway."

"You slept with her?"

I nod, suddenly feeling like the world's biggest heel. Did I take advantage of her? No, she'd practically thrown herself at me and said she wanted to repay me. Of course, that wasn't necessary, but I still took her virginity.

"Regrets?" Enzo asks.

I think over his question for a long minute. Did I regret spending the night with that beautiful woman and taking her innocence? "No," I state. "But the problem is...fuck, I don't know. I'm so confused."

Enzo takes a sip of his whiskey and studies me over the rim of his glass. "What are you confused about? It sounds like you met someone that you actually like. Spend some time with her and get to know her better."

But, I shake my head. "I can't."

"Why not?"

I huff out a frustrated breath and shove a hand through my hair. "Because! Wanting to be with her involves opening myself up to be hurt again. I can't do that," I grit out. "I won't."

Getting over Cynda was the hardest thing I'd ever done and her betrayal had scorched me and left a deep scar.

"You can't compare every woman you meet to Cynda," Enzo says in a quiet, careful voice. He knows he best tread lightly when it comes to this subject. My whole family knows and I never discuss what happened. Not fucking ever.

"Easier said than done."

"It sounds to me like you want to spend time with Hannah, but you're fighting yourself on it."

"Oh, I'll be spending a helluva lot of time with her. If she accepts my job offer."

"You offered her a job?"

"As my new assistant," I explain. "Miceli said I needed someone, and Hannah needs a better job. It makes sense."

"And she hasn't accepted?" Enzo's mouth quirks up in a smirk. "Why not?"

"I don't know. Maybe because I took her virginity last night and then turned into a first-class bastard this morning."

"Aww, fuck, Vin. What did you do?"

"Woke up, questioned everything, panicked and then took her straight home." I scrub a hand over my face. "Not my best moment."

"No, it doesn't sound like it." He turns his glass in a circle. "Most women don't appreciate being kicked out immediately after sex."

"I didn't kick her out!" He arches a brow. "I sort of scooted her out."

"Same thing, man."

I let out a weary sigh. "I'm a damn idiot. But I don't know what to do now."

"Stop focusing on the potential negatives. Be happy and enjoy life for once. Indulge. If it goes somewhere then great and if not, then oh well. Don't let yourself be so hung up on Cynda still. That's all in the past. Time to move on to greener pastures."

It's easy for Enzo to give advice, I realize, because he's never had his heart broken before. But I do want to be happy. And Hannah makes me laugh and smile. The urge to get to know her better fills me. But am I brave enough to do it? To take a chance?

I just don't know if I can.

"Stop debating over every little thing that can go wrong and go call your girl," Enzo encourages me. He swallows back the rest of his whiskey. "Now I gotta go stop by the office."

"On Sunday?"

"Every day is a work day, Vin," he says, slapping a palm down on the table and standing up. "There's no such thing as relaxing on the weekend when it comes to making money."

"You know what they say—all work and no play…"

"You find me someone to play with and maybe I'll consider taking Sundays off." He tosses me a salute, throws a wad of cash on the table and says, "Drinks are on me. Now go fix this situation with Hannah by at least getting her to agree to be your assistant. Okay?"

I nod then watch my brother walk out. Every single pair of female eyes follows him and I roll my own eyes. He could have every woman in this city eating out of his hand if he wanted. Maybe one day he'll look around and take his pick. But, probably not anytime soon. He's too wrapped up in increasing the family fortune.

Plucking my phone out of my jacket, I can't resist the temptation to call Hannah any longer. Of course, I'm calling her because, goddammit, I want to hear her voice. But I'm going to pretend it's more about the job offer than the simple fact I'm jonesing to hear my angel's voice.

"Vin?"

The moment she answers, I know something isn't right. She sounds out of breath and even a little scared.

"Hannah, what's wrong?" I immediately ask, straightening up to my full height and instantly in tune with her fear. "Are you okay?"

"Um, I don't know. I mean, yes, I think so."

"Where are you? What's going on?"

"That guy from the auction just showed up out of nowhere."

The blood in my body freezes. "What?" I hiss.

"Caleb Durant. He wanted me to get in his car, but I said no. I'm hurrying back to my apartment right now—"

"I'm coming. Listen carefully. I want you to stay on the line with me, okay? I'm coming to you. How far are you from your place?"

"Maybe ten minutes? I took a walk, trying to clear my head."

"I'm on my way, Angel. Just keep walking and I'll find you, okay?"

"Okay," she whispers, and I have the impression she's clutching onto the phone, holding it to her ear like a lifeline.

Heart in my throat, I hit the gas and fly over to Brooklyn in record time. Luckily, it doesn't take me too long because I was already fairly close and I find Hannah almost to her apartment. Pulling the car over, I throw the door open. "Hannah!"

The moment she hears my voice, she stops and jumps in, pulling the door shut and locking it. "I'm so glad to see you," she gushes and my chest tightens. "For a minute, I thought he was following me, but I don't know."

The fear in her voice makes me tighten my grip on the steering wheel and want to beat the living shit out of Caleb Durant. "You're sure you're okay?" I ask, prying my hand loose from its steel grip around the wheel and snagging hers.

"I am now," she reassures me.

"No one is going to hurt you," I tell her. The feel of her small hand in mind settles my mind. I have her. She's safe. No one is taking her from me. "I promise."

And I mean it. From this point forward, I'm taking Hannah Everson under my protection. Whether she likes it or not.

11

HANNAH

Instead of driving me home, I notice Vin turns the car toward his place. I'm about to object, but something inside of me doesn't want to. The truth is I want to be with him. Running into Caleb like that, out in the wild, put me on edge. Even more so, I missed Vin and I just want to be near him again.

God, am I turning into a pathetic, needy woman after one night with the man? Technically, I slept beside him the last two nights. Of course, not much sleeping occurred in his bed, but lying in his arms, breathing in his citrusy scent and feeling the steady rise and fall of his chest beneath my cheek did something to me. It made me want more. So much more.

But after the way he closed off this morning, I began having massive doubts. While I'm sitting here hoping to spend more time with him, Vin closed off and rushed me straight back to my apartment. After the intense night we had, his actions left me confused and hurt. The moment I needed him, though, he came running straight to me. That has to mean something, right?

I'm not sure where we stand or what he wants, but I'll never forget how Vin is always there for me when I need someone the most. After losing my mom, I've had no one else in my life to rely on. Maybe now I do? The idea makes my heart swell with hope and something more. Something I'm too scared to even consider since I've only known him since Friday night.

By the time we arrive at Vin's apartment, I've settled down and I'm more relaxed. He parks in the underground garage and we take the elevator up to his floor. I'm not sure what to say and he has a grim, steely look on his face, so neither of us says anything. Once we're safely inside, he locks the door and turns to me.

"I want you to tell me exactly what happened."

Shifting uneasily, trying to read his mood, I nod. I suppose it's the least I can do after he came to my rescue for a second time. "Well, it's like I told you. I had just left the cemetery—"

"Cemetery?"

"Um, yeah," I say, twisting my hands and feeling my cheeks flush. "Sometimes I walk down to visit my mom. I like to sit there and talk to her. It probably sounds silly to you."

"No, not at all." His voice drops. "Losing her was really hard on you, wasn't it?"

"She was my best friend," I whisper, doing my best to force back the tears and failing miserably. *Dammit.* Squeezing my eyes shut, I try to regain control of my emotions, but it's so damn hard. Losing her is still so raw and sometimes I can't help bursting into tears.

Vin immediately pulls me close, wrapping an arm around my lower back while the other holds my cheek to his chest. I melt into him and let the tears flow. A few minutes later, I sniffle against his nice white shirt, pull back and realize I got it all wet. An embarrassing combination of tears and snot.

"I'm sorry." I immediately try to brush it dry, but that doesn't work. I'm probably just making it worse.

"It's fine," he murmurs, his big hand still stroking up and down my back. "It's just a shirt."

When I can't seem to stop wiping at the spot, he grabs my hand, forcing it to stop, and lifts it to his mouth. Then he presses a soft kiss to my knuckles. Our gazes lock and my stomach fills with butterflies.

"Will you stay for dinner?" he asks huskily.

I can't look away from his amazing green eyes and I nod.

"Good." Vin releases my hand, leans in and kisses me. It's soft, tender and over before I'd like. "Want to help me make some lasagna? Maybe toss a salad?"

"Yes," I whisper, a little wobbly after the touch of his lips on mine.

We walk into the large, modern kitchen and he nods to a chair at the marble-topped island. "Have a seat and I'll pour us some wine. I think we could both use a glass while you finish telling me what happened with Caleb Durant."

I couldn't agree more. My nerves are still frazzled by the incident. But watching Vin move around the kitchen, pour us wine and start pulling out pots, pans and ingredients sets my mind and heart at ease. He has this calm energy that speaks to me and reassures me on a soul-deep level.

I tell Vin how I had stepped out of the cemetery gates and then Caleb pulled up out of nowhere in his flashy BMW. "He said things didn't turn out like he'd planned."

"I'm sure," Vin says dryly. I can't help but notice how tightly he's holding his wine glass and I watch him take a long, aggravated sip. "Then what happened?"

"He said he wanted to get to know me better, introduced himself and it's almost like he waited for my reaction. Like I should recognize his name or something."

"I checked with brother Enzo who knows everyone worth knowing and he said Caleb Durant thinks he's a bigshot in the finance world," Vin explained, a sour look on his face. "He's not."

"I told him I had to go and started walking. He still thought my name was Mary."

"Did you correct him?"

"No."

"Good girl."

"He asked if he could give me a ride and I said no. I think that made him mad because then he got snippy. I didn't want to encourage him, though. He ended up peeling away. I'm sure that's most likely the end of it and I probably made the whole thing into a much bigger deal than it really is."

"He harassed you," Vin said, voice steely. "It *is* a big deal and I won't let it happen again."

"Thank you, Vin," I say softly. Knowing he is looking out for me means everything. I slide off the stool and walk around, looking over all the ingredients. "I'll make the salad."

"Sounds good. I have a fresh loaf of French bread, too, if you'd like me to whip up some garlic bread."

"Wow, you seem pretty good in the kitchen." *And in the bedroom,* I think wickedly, pressing my lips together as I reach for the greens.

"My mom made sure all her kids knew how to at least cook lasagna. Some of us are better than others, but I'm pretty decent. I can make some mean manicotti, too."

I chuckle. "Tell me about your family. Is it big?"

"I have an older brother named Miceli. Then there's me, Enzo, Angelo and our baby sister Carlotta—who you met the other day. I told her to send the dress with a courier, but she's so damn nosy. I should've known she'd show up herself to deliver it."

"I'm glad I got to meet her, even just briefly. She seems sweet."

"She can be a handful," he informs me with a grin as he chops a fresh tomato. "But we love her. Then my parents live in Sicily on the vineyard."

"I bet it's beautiful. Do you get back there often?"

"The entire family goes every Christmas. Sicily is amazing during the holidays."

"Do you speak Italian?" I ask, cocking my head. He has no trace of an accent and it never occurred to me until now.

"We all do. Fluently."

"Really?" For whatever reason that amazes me. And impresses the hell out of me. Most people in America only speak one language—English. "Say something."

His lips edge up in a smirk and then a slew of beautiful, low-spoken Italian words spill from his mouth. My jaw drops and my panties are instantly soaked. It's the sexiest damn thing I've ever heard.

"What did you just say?" I ask, a little breathless and completely turned on.

"Come closer and I'll tell you."

Heart in my throat, I set the parmesan cheese down and move closer. Vin brushes my hair back off my shoulder, leans down and whispers in my ear, "I said you're absolutely stunning. A bright, golden light that washes away the darkness. So good, so pure. I want your light to consume me, my Angel."

Oh, God. I let out a shaky breath and then lose my mind a little. Desire infuses me and I turn my head. Popping up onto my toes, I slam my mouth against his hard and fast. I don't think he expects the move and he groans into my mouth as I kiss him passionately. After a little bit, Vin slides his hands through my hair, cupping the back of my neck and takes control, deepening the kiss. Commanding. Controlling. Making me want him on a primitive level I never knew existed.

Walking me backwards, devouring me, his tongue explores and caresses every square inch of my mouth. My rear end bumps into the table. Before I realize what's happening, Vin pushes forward, maneuvering himself between my legs, and forces me to lay back on the tabletop. He's on top of me, kissing me desperately, and reaches for my leggings. In one fell swoop, my leggings and panties get tossed. Then his hand is between my legs, caressing, spreading my juices over my folds and up around my clit.

With a cry, my head drops back against the table and my hips push against his hand. He slides two fingers into my soaked channel while his thumb massages my clit until I'm squeezing my thighs together and biting my lip to keep from screaming.

"Spread your legs, Angel," he rasps, thrusting his fingers in and out. Forcing my thighs apart. He's working me into a frenzy and I feel my control slip away. The orgasm hits me hard and waves of pleasure spread through my body. Before I can even begin to recover, Vin flips me over and I'm lying face down. My heart thunders as he leans over and whispers, "I'm going to take you like this, *Angioletto.* Sink deep into your sweet, wet pussy. Can I do that? Fuck you deep?"

"Yes...please," I beg, pushing my ass back against him. I hear his zipper go down and the crinkle of a condom packet. I have no idea where he got it from so quickly and I don't care. I just want to feel his big cock inside me.

I get my wish almost immediately. Vin grabs my hips, fingers digging into my flesh, hikes my ass up and sinks into me from behind. We both moan and the sensation of him stretching and filling me is almost too much to bear. It stings at first but then my body adjusts to the new position, welcoming him deeper as he begins to thrust. Sinking in and out of me.

"So fucking good," he rasps, grunting with each thrust. "Fuck, you're tight. You squeeze me so good...so goddamn wet..."

I turn my cheek, laying it against the cool surface of the table and try to hold on as Vin begins to move faster...harder. He's pounding into me and his hand finds its way beneath my body, zeroing in on my clit. Pressing, massaging, rolling the aching nub until I can't take it anymore. A scream tears from my throat and I buck hard as my release rocks through my body. Like a bolt of lightning it zaps and sears straight through me, setting everything on fire. The entire table lurches forward with the force of Vin's thrusts. Then he groans, stiffens above me and I feel a long shudder rack through the length of his frame as he orgasms. He hisses something in Italian then drops down on top of me. He's careful not to crush me and when he presses his lips against my shoulder, I let out a shaky sigh.

When he finally peels himself off me, I can't move. I'm breathing hard, unable to lift my head up. I can't believe that I just had sex with Vin on the kitchen table. Backwards. Oh, my God. He makes me lose every rational thought in my head when we're together. I like him so damn much. Hell, it's time to be honest with myself. It's so much more than like. I want so badly to call this man my significant other. I want to go to bed with him, have fantastic, mind-blowing sex all night long, then I want to wake up in his arms every morning. It's like he's cast some sort of magical spell over me.

Or, maybe my pussy.

No, it's more than that. I want to meet his family and go to Sicily with him on Christmas. I want him to teach me Italian and give me babies.

Holy shit. The first man I sleep with, I'm falling in love with. I'm not sure what to do with that. But, I need to be careful. One minute he's all in and the next, he cools off. Rolling over on the table, I look up and he's staring down at me, a strange look in his vibrant green eyes. Vin extends his hand and I take it with zero hesitation.

"I didn't...hurt you, did I?" He caresses a hand down my bare hip and I shiver.

"No."

Vin nods, moving his hand around and circling his fingertips on my lower back. "I didn't mean to be so intense. It's like I lost all control."

"I liked it," I admit shyly.

Heat flares in his expression, lighting his emerald eyes afire, and a muscle flexes in his cheek. "Are you coming to work for me tomorrow?" he asks.

"Yes," I whisper, knowing it's the wisest decision.

A huge smile lights up his handsome face.

"But..."

"No buts," he murmurs and kisses me softly.

I enjoy the feel of our mouths moving together longer than I should. Placing a hand against his chest, I push him back and he frowns. "But," I repeat firmly, "if I'm going to be your employee, we can't be sleeping together."

There. I said it. Now the ball is in his court and all I want to hear is him say screw it then and that he wants me to be his girlfriend rather than his assistant.

Instead, a hooded look comes over his bright green eyes. He doesn't seem very thrilled with my answer, but he doesn't offer me an alternative, either. My heart sinks slightly, but I put on a strong outward appearance.

"We need to set some ground rules," I tell him, deciding to be tough with him. The alternative is me winding up with a broken heart and I don't want that. I need to protect myself. Seeing him every day in a professional environment means we need to act like professionals. Otherwise, things could get sticky fast. I also don't want the other employees to judge and think the only reason I'm there is because I'm fucking the boss. That doesn't sit well with me at all.

"What rules?" he growls, not looking happy.

I wave a hand between us. "This has to stop. As much as I enjoy being with you..." I clear my throat, flushing, "I'm a professional. I don't want people thinking you only hired me because you consider me a piece of ass."

"I don't think that," he hisses vehemently. "I'm hiring you because I believe it's a good decision and you're going to be a hard-working and competent employee."

"Good. Otherwise, I wouldn't be able to work for you." Again, he narrows his eyes, glaring. "I just want to make sure we're on the same page."

"Fine," he grits out. "Let's finish dinner."

And just like that I've lost him. Something in the air changes and I have no idea how we went from a scorching fuck on the kitchen table to this...to nothing. At this point, I don't even know if we're friends. My heart hurts as I reach for the salad bowl and begin to toss the greens.

A part of me still holds out, hoping he will tell me to forget the job and be his girlfriend. But he doesn't. And that devastates me more than I care to admit.

You barely just met the guy, I try to tell myself. *Get over it.*

But that's so much easier said than done.

From this point forward, I know our relationship will be strictly professional and platonic—and no matter how difficult it will be for me, I know it's the right thing to do.

12

VIN

I know she's right. She shouldn't be sleeping with the boss at her new job. But I don't think my dick got the memo. Of course, I agree with her, but that doesn't mean I'm happy about it. Nevertheless, come Monday morning, I'm determined to play the consummate professional. I'm not going to notice the way her slim skirt fits her ass so perfectly or the glimpse of a pink satin bra strap beneath her blouse or the sexy sway of her hips when she walks across the office in those high heels.

Nope. Not gonna pay any attention, I remind myself, eyes glued to her talking to another employee. She laughs and tosses her blonde hair over a shoulder and I stifle a groan. I've been hard all day, wanting to drag her into my office, lock the door, hike that skirt up and bend her over my desk.

Squeezing my eyes shut, I don't see how this is going to work. How can I handle being in such close proximity with her every single day, but not being able to touch her. It's sheer torture.

Later that afternoon, Hannah is in my office and she's standing next to me, leaning far too close, and asking me questions about how to read a financial summary report. Her baby powder scent fills my nose and she looks so damn sexy. I love the fact that she wants to learn and do a good job, but she's killing me. By the time five o'clock rolls around, I'm ready to lose my mind.

Unlike Enzo, I don't enjoy working twenty-four hours a day. So when it's time to leave, I encourage everyone to go home. I'm not the kind of boss to stay at the office until eight o'clock at night and expect everyone else to follow suit. As long as things are under control and in good shape, whatever work is left will be there when we come back tomorrow. Besides, the company is in excellent shape and making a hefty profit. Our board members are raking in the bucks and positively thrilled. Rossi Vineyard is and always has been a very profitable company and I'm happy to be steering us toward even more success.

I'm about to offer Hannah a ride home when my phone rings. It's Miceli and I answer because I know he's going to want to know how today went. I might be new when it comes to showing up at the office every day, but I'm very familiar with Rossi Vineyard and how it runs. I've actually been making a lot of important decisions behind the scenes and helped increase the revenue, so it only made sense that I was officially named President of the company. That's one thing I love about my family—they like to give credit where credit is due. They reward hard work and make others feel appreciated.

Being the second son in a mafia family hasn't always been easy. As the eldest, Miceli handles the sticky situations and sits on the throne, making decisions that I'd rather not. But, lately, things have been changing. We might run a large majority of this city, but we're not the only ones. There are five families constantly vying for power and control. The Five Families are made up of the Rossi's, The Bianchi's, The DeLuca's, The Caparelli's and The Milano's.

Up until recently, Miceli has been the only one to deal directly with the other families when it comes to going to meetings and making important decisions. The whole organization is quite civilized and we each have an area of the city that we are in charge of. Is it perfect? No, of course not. Are there fights and jealousy? Sure. But, for the most part, we work together when it comes to defeating and conquering our enemies. Ultimately, we know if the five of us aren't on top then someone else will be. So, it's important that we watch each other's backs at all times and keep the lines of communication open.

This isn't *The Godfather*. But, if someone crosses the line, it can become brutal fast.

Not too long ago, Miceli and Rocco Bianche came to blows over my brother's wife, Alessia. Rocco ended up dead and that changed the dynamics of the Five Families. Instead of only the oldest figurehead representing each family and making all of the decisions, it's evolved. Now we are all invited to attend meetings and be a part of the decision-making process and the voting. I'm not quite as involved in all of that drama as Miceli and much prefer to focus on Rossi Vineyard.

"Hey, Miceli," I answer. The moment I greet my brother, Hannah appears in the doorway looking as delicious as a piece of creamy cannoli. One I want to sink my teeth into and savor. "Hold on."

Lowering my phone, I look over at her. "Everything okay?" I ask.

"Is there anything else you need before I go?"

Yeah, how about a blowjob? Gritting my back molars, I shake my head. "No, but thanks. I can give you a ride home—" *I can give you a different kind of ride, too. A hot, sweaty, hard ride that'll make you scream.*

"Oh, no, that's not necessary. I need to pick up some groceries and I'll just grab an Uber. Thank you, though. Today was good."

I smile, glad to hear she's happy. Hannah being happy makes me happy. "See you tomorrow then." Even though it's going to eventually kill me.

"See you tomorrow," she says. "And thank you, Vin. I really like it here."

"I'm glad."

Hannah tosses me an adorable wave and I watch her walk away, until she disappears from view. I think I may have just drooled and I swipe a hand over the corner of my mouth.

"Miceli? Sorry."

"Wow," Miceli says. "I never thought I'd see the day."

"What're you talking about?" I ask, instantly growing cranky because I know he's about to say something to annoy me. I can tell by his teasing tone.

"Was that your new assistant you offered to give a ride home to?" He bursts out laughing and I mentally curse him. "Who did you hire?"

I drop my head and pinch the bridge of my nose. "I could use a drink. Any interest in joining me?"

"Sure," he says, still chuckling. "Let me tell Alessia and I'll meet you over at Adaggio's. I want to hear all about this mystery woman."

Rolling my eyes, I disconnect the call and sigh. Enzo already knows about Hannah so I may as well tell Miceli, too. However, when I arrive at Adaggio's it's not just Miceli waiting for me. All of my brothers and Carlotta are there.

"What the hell, Miceli? I didn't know this was going to be a family affair." I pull a chair out and plunk down in the seat with a pouty face.

"Look, we can help," Enzo says.

I grab a passing waiter and order a glass of red wine. I have a feeling they're all about to gang up on me and I'm going to need some alcohol to deal with the situation.

"First off, we're all aware of Hannah," Angelo states.

"How? I only told Enzo." I send my younger brother a glare.

"And me," Carlotta reminds me pleasantly. "He asked me to pick out a dress for her and I hand delivered it. Hannah is a doll. She's so pretty and pleasant and young. Younger than me."

When Lottie winks at me, I close my hands into fists, telling myself not to strangle her. My sister has never been one to keep a secret and she probably blabbed about Hannah to Ang and Miceli.

"How's she working out as your new assistant?" Enzo asks, a wicked gleam in his eyes.

"Are you mixing business with pleasure?" Angelo teases, waggling his eyebrows.

"You guys are all a bunch of fuckers," I grumble and take a long sip of the wine the waiter just set down in front of me. After they order some appetizers to split, the interrogation starts up again.

"How old is Hannah exactly?" Angelo asks.

"She's twenty-two," I admit. There's no point in lying; my family will find out the truth. They're like a bunch of private investigators when they want to figure something out.

"Yep, younger than me," Lottie says.

I roll my eyes. "But she's more mature than you," I fire back.

"Oh, I doubt that." She sends me a smirk and then plucks the cherry from her amaretto sour.

As much as I love my little sister, good luck to whoever she winds up with. Some man is going to have a damn handful to deal with one of these days.

"Okay, I want details," Miceli announces. "What the hell did I miss? How did you meet this woman?"

I glance over at Enzo. "There was a private auction and Enzo had an invite which he gave to me. He thought I might be able to meet someone there." I keep my story PG-rated since Lottie is here. She doesn't need to know my only intention was to find a woman to hook up with. As worldly as she tries to be, Carlotta is an innocent with very limited experience when it comes to men and relationships. I suppose having four older brothers involved in the mafia is a little intimidating and keeps most potential suitors far away.

"Are you talking about the White Auction? The sex auction?" Miceli asks bluntly. Beside him, Lottie gasps.

I roll my eyes. "I didn't know it was a sex auction. I thought there were going to be paintings or sculptures. Shit like that. Not women on a stage and men bidding."

"That's disgusting," Carlotta says, wrinkling her nose. "She turns her attention to Enzo. "You go to sex auctions?"

"No! I had no idea about that." Enzo lifts his hands. "I swear. I'd been getting the invitation to attend, but I'm always too busy to go and I throw it out. I gave it to Vin and told him to go and meet someone. I didn't know what really went on there."

"Everybody knows what goes on there," Miceli says in a flat voice.

"I didn't!" Enzo and I say at the exact same time.

Miceli and Angelo chuckle.

"Okay, so what happened?" Angelo presses. "You bought a girl?"

"It wasn't like that," I insist. "Hannah was forced to do it because she owed money to Dexter Creed. She didn't want to be up there so when a couple of creeps started bidding on her virginity, I stepped in and offered more money."

"How much?" Miceli asks.

"Yeah, what did you end up paying?" Enzo chimes in.

I clear my throat and take another sip of wine. "One-hundred and fifty six thousand."

Everyone's eyes go wide.

"Dollars?" Angelo splutters.

"No, pesos," I answer dryly.

"Tell me you fucked her."

"Jesus, Ang!" Carlotta slaps Angelo's shoulder. "Don't be a pig."

"Well, that's a lot of money to pay, and if there's no return—"

"Okay, stop," I interrupt. "Nothing happened that night. She was scared and upset. All I wanted to do was get her out of there. Comfort her, you know?"

"*That* night?"

Leave it to the ever perceptive Miceli to catch that slip. I sigh and say, "We've gotten closer since then."

"Make sure you get your money's worth," Angelo says.

"Oh, my God, Angelo!" Carlotta whacks him again.

"What?" He shrugs, rubbing his shoulder where she punched him.

"How much do you like this woman?" Miceli asks.

"Enough to hire her as his assistant," Enzo comments. "But are you keeping things professional?"

"That's the problem. I think hiring her might've been a mistake because I can't think straight when she's around. I've never wanted a woman as much as I want Hannah. It's like she's bewitched me or something crazy."

Miceli gives me a knowing nod. "Or something."

"What do you mean?" I ask. He's the only one of us who's fallen in love and gotten married. If anyone understands, it has to be him and I'm desperate for advice. For clarity. Because I have no fucking idea what's going on right now or how to handle the situation.

"Sounds to me like you're falling for her. Falling hard," Miceli says knowingly.

I immediately shake my head. "No. No, I'm not."

"Vin, that's a good thing," Carlotta interjects. "Don't fight it. You deserve to find someone who's going to treat you well."

My eyes narrow and thoughts of Cynda and our failed relationship flood my head. "I don't do relationships. You all know that. Not after *her*," I add harshly. I refuse to even say her damn name aloud.

"Not everyone is like her," Carlotta states.

"No. Relationships," I repeat firmly.

"Maybe you should think about it," Enzo says. The appetizers arrive and my siblings dig in, but I've lost my appetite. Instead, I order another glass of wine.

"There's nothing to think about."

"Do you have any idea what Hannah wants?" Miceli asks.

"Yeah," I say bitterly. "She says now that we're working together, things need to remain professional. She doesn't want anyone to believe she's sleeping with the boss."

"Good for her," Carlotta says, swiping up a piece of bruschetta. "She has morals. I like that."

Hmm. I don't say anything, but a part of me wishes that she didn't. No, that's not right. I'm glad she's a hard worker and wants to do a good job. But, I also don't want to give up the sex. It's too damn good with her.

"Sounds like you're in quite the pickle, big bro," Angelo says, munching on some toasted ravioli. "And I don't envy you at all. Good luck."

"Gee, thanks, Ang." *My little brother, the player.* He has no clue what it's like to fall for a woman. To fall deeply in love and then have your heart torn out and shredded when she cheats on you. It's why I've erected these walls and will hide behind them until the day I die.

I'm not sure how else to protect myself.

My mind goes to Hannah and I remember how frightened she was when Caleb Durant stopped her. "Hey, have any of you guys dealt with Caleb Durant? Enzo, I know you said he's a wannabe, but what else do we know?"

Miceli and Enzo exchange a look that speaks volumes.

"He's a dick," Enzo states.

"Yeah, I had the misfortune of dealing with the man once before," Miceli adds, chomping on a piece of bruschetta. "He's a snake on a powertrip and can't be trusted."

Good to know.

"He's the one who tried to win Hannah. Then he approached her the other day, trying to coax her into his car."

"Eww," Lottie says.

"That's one way of describing him," Enzo says. "He's a pain in the ass and, for whatever reason, thinks he's some kind of big shot. Trust me, he's not."

Between Enzo and Miceli, my brothers know the biggest players in town and we give respect where it's due. However, Caleb Durant sounds like a slimy asshole who may need to be dealt with. Plus, I'd take great joy in knocking him down a few pegs. Because if he so much as looks at Hannah again, I'm going to beat the living shit out of him.

"There's a meeting with the Five Families next week," Miceli informs us. "Are you all coming?"

Even though I'd rather not, I nod my head. Maybe I can claim I have things to do with the winery that day and get out of it. Sometimes the drama between the five most powerful families in NYC is too much for me.

"Also, send me the latest reports on the winery, Vin. Business is booming and I know you're going to make it even better over there now that you're running things."

His faith in me means a lot. "Well, we're all running things and making decisions together," I remind him modestly.

"Yeahh, but you're handling the day to day bullshit and that means a lot. Thank you for taking the position."

I nod, grateful for the opportunity.

As we wrap up drinks and finish off the food, Angelo gives me the side eye. "So, when do we get to meet your new woman? The mysterious Hannah."

"Never. And she's not my woman," I instantly say, getting defensive.

"Isn't she?" Miceli asks, eyeing me closely. I frown because, as usual, the man is far too damn perceptive.

But I brush them off with a shrug, not wanting to get into my mix of crazy emotions and how Hannah is everything I want, but I'm too scared to make her mine. Besides, what's the point of them meeting her when she's not my girlfriend? And she never will be.

I grit my teeth, realizing just how much that thought bothers me.

13

HANNAH

Working on the corporate side of Rossi Vineyard is unlike any job I've ever had before. Normally, I'm on my feet all day and running around like a mad woman, trying to please customers at the diner, most of them cranky and cheap tippers. But the office environment here is laidback and everyone is so nice.

Well, everyone except Vin. For whatever reason, every time I come around—which is a lot because I'm his assistant—he gets a pole up his ass. It's not that he isn't professional toward me. He is. Very much so. But I can't help but notice he's getting grumpier and grumpier every day. I've been working with him for three weeks now and have done everything to be the best assistant possible to him. I answer his phone, schedule his appointments, talk to the distributors, make coffee and do lunch runs, and so much more. He even told me he's giving me a bonus. Yet something seems to be bothering him.

Today, I'm not sure what crawled up his ass and died, but he's in a *mood*. A very sour one. No matter what I do, he's getting annoyed and seems vexed about every little thing. I'm not sure if it's me or he's got something else going on that's upsetting him. But, I've never seen him so…bothered.

The truth is I miss the relationship we had when we first met. But sleeping with the boss isn't who I am. So, instead, I'll do my best to keep up with his mood swings.

My phone buzzes and I see Vin's number flash on the screen. "Hi," I say, not meaning to sound so out of breath. But he makes me feel all so sultry and sexy. "What do you need?"

Shit. The double entendre isn't lost on me. I pull my lower lip into my mouth and meet his eyes through the glass. My desk faces his office and his blinds are wide open. He's staring at me...hungrily?

"Can you come in here?" he rasps, shifting in his chair.

"Sure." I hang up the receiver, stand up and smooth my skirt down. It's important that I dress up for work now and, since I'm making way more money than ever before, I treated myself to a shopping spree. It was so nice not to stress over having to buy new clothes and to simply enjoy picking out a whole new wardrobe. I really enjoy getting to dress up in skirts and dresses every day. High heels, too. It makes me feel more sophisticated and I do not miss my apron or old shoes I used to wear at the diner. I feel so much fancier now and the fact that I'm helping Vin makes me happy.

Although, he doesn't look very happy at the moment. He looks almost uncomfortable. Stepping into his office, I breeze up to his desk and smile at him. "What do you need, Mr. Rossi?" I ask, trailing my fingers along the edge of his desk.

Okay, so maybe I'm taking the formal thing a little too far. But this is my first professional job in the workforce. I want to give a good impression.

Something flashes over his face and I notice his hand tighten around the pen he's holding. "You don't have to address me so formally," he reminds me. "I've told you that."

"I know, but it's fun."

"It's not fun," he grumbles. "It makes me feel old and sounds like we barely know each other. Call me Vin."

"Okay, sorry...Vin." My attention zeroes in on the stack of papers in front of him. "Do you need any copies of anything? Or, how about anything mailed? I could walk down to the post office—"

"Actually, I could use another coffee."

"I'll run down and grab you one."

He reaches for his wallet, pulls out a twenty-dollar bill and hands it over to me. The moment our hands touch, it's like a shock zips between us, jolting through me with electric force. I yank my hand back then automatically meet his intense gaze. His eyes are like two swirling pools of green heat and I squeeze my thighs together because I remember that look only too well.

Vin Rossi wants me. And, I mean as more than just his assistant. But it's not a line we can cross. That's what I keep telling myself anyway.

Vin clears his throat. "When you get back, I need your help with some marketing decisions."

My brows shoot up. "Marketing decisions?" I echo. That's placing a lot of trust in me when I don't have any experience other than running errands and simple tasks.

"You have a good eye and I want to hear your opinion on some things we're rebranding."

I can't help but stand a little taller. "Okay. Be back soon." Turning around, I walk out of the office with a pep in my step. This is exactly what I was hoping for—a chance to prove I'm smart and a quick learner. One day, I'd love to move up and take on a more challenging position. But, for now, I enjoy working so closely with Vin even though he hasn't smiled at me much lately.

There's a coffee shop located right in our building on the first floor, so I take the elevator down and grab Vin his usual espresso and myself an ice-blended mocha. It only takes less than ten minutes before I'm back upstairs and handing him his drink.

"Thank you. C'mon, let's go into the conference room."

I take a sip of my drink and walk with Vin down the hallway. Once we're inside the conference room, he shuts the door. The large glass wall that faces the lobby is covered by blinds and they're pulled tightly closed. It's just me and him in here, and I walk over to the long, dark wood conference table which is covered with artwork and logo designs for several of the bottles of wine. I pick a picture up and study it.

"Is this for a new line?" I ask.

"It is." He steps closer, his shoulder brushing mine. "I'd like your opinion on all the images and I want to know which ones are your favorites. And, of course, which ones don't work."

The amount of trust he's putting in me is thrilling. After another quick sip, I set my drink aside, away from all the artwork, and lean over, examining each picture closely. I can feel Vin's gaze on me as I study them all and make comments about each one. We go back and forth, pointing out the pros and cons, debating over what works best for the Rossi Vineyard brand. In the end, we're on exactly the same page and we both like the design with a sun setting over a vineyard.

"It's perfect," I say, elbows on the table. Vin is standing so close, his thigh practically touching my hip, and I briefly close my eyes and pray for strength. We've been so close for the past hour and it's getting too hard to ignore his tempting citrus scent or the way his warm body brushes against mine or his low voice in my ear. I have a feeling he's struggling, too, and when he moves behind me and grasps my hips, I whimper.

He's about to pounce.

"Vin…" I try to protest, but the words are stuck in my throat. I'm still bent over the table, propped up on my elbows.

"I need you, Hannah. Christ, I can't stand being this close to you and not being able to take you in my arms. It's killing me," he rasps.

Suddenly, I have no control over my actions. I push my ass back against his pelvis and feel how hard he is, how badly he wants me. My hips circle of their own accord, pushing against his straining cock. Teasing him until he's rocking against me, too. His warm hands reach for the hem of my skirt and begin sliding it up. Then his hand moves between my legs, shoves the damp fabric of my panties aside, and his finger sinks deep inside me.

"Oh, God," I moan, pushing back, my hips gyrating as I ride his hand. He slips another finger inside my slick channel and his other hand reaches around to play with my clit. "Vin!"

He's leaning over me, kissing and licking the side of my neck, and it's all too much. I'm aching for him and the tension is building hard and fast.

"Please," I moan.

"Please, what, *Angioletto?*" he whispers, circling his tongue over the crest of my ear.

"I want you inside me."

He speeds up the thrust of his fingers, increases the pressure on my clit and I go hurling off the edge as a powerful orgasm rips through me, making my entire body shake. With a gasp, I drop my forehead against the table and shiver as delicious waves of pleasure ripple through me.

I'm so wet and half-delirious for Vin's cock when, suddenly, there's a rap at the door.

"Fuck," Vin hisses, stepping back and hurriedly re-zipping his pants.

I'm still dazed as he pulls me up off the table and smooths my skirt back down. "Hang on. I'll get rid of whoever it is." He presses a quick kiss against my temple and I drop down in a chair, utterly spent.

I watch him hobble over to the door and open it a crack. His low, yet quite audible swear, hits my ears and I try to see who's there. With great reluctance, Vin opens the door all the way up and three of the best-looking men I've ever seen come striding into the conference room.

Oh, God. I sit up straighter and try to look like I didn't just get finger-fucked by Vin on the conference room table. *So much for being professional,* I think dryly.

"Well, hello," the one in a sharp designer suit says, smiling from ear to ear. "I'm Vin's brother Enzo and, I assume, you're the lovely Hannah I've heard so much about."

My eyes widen and Vin growls a warning, but they don't seem to pay any attention. *Has Vin really been talking about me?* I wonder.

I stand up and shake Enzo's hand.

"I'm Miceli," the tallest, biggest one of them states in a gravelly voice.

"It's nice to meet you," I say and shake his hand. Then I look at the last one who has a wicked-looking grin on his handsome face.

"And I'm Angelo." As we shake hands, I try not to flush as he looks from me to Vin. "You two are looking awfully…satisfied."

My face turns beet red and I hear Vin mumble under his breath, "Not really."

Oh, God, how embarrassing. They must know we were right in the middle of messing around. How? We're both flushed, I suppose, and then my gaze drops to the way Vin is standing, his suit jacket now buttoned up and covering his crotch. Oh. He's clearly hiding a massive erection. But they wouldn't know that. They must just know their brother too well.

Still, it doesn't make the situation any less humiliating for either of us.

What I really appreciate, though, is nobody dwells on it. After that very minor teasing, the brothers sit down at the table and, to my surprise, Vin invites me to join them. I sit down beside him and he immediately starts talking about how we came up with our top picks for the rebranding project. After some minor debating, they all agree on the design we chose.

Honestly, I feel so good, so useful, and I sit up taller beside Vin. He gives me all the credit and tells them I have an amazing eye. Then he mentions placing me in a position in the marketing department in the future.

"But, I'm not ready to give her up as my assistant quite yet." Beneath the table, his hand brushes against mine then his fingers wrap around my hand, squeezing.

All I can do is smile. He makes me feel so worthy and such an important part of this team. I appreciate it more than words can say and I squeeze his hand back in answer.

"Okay, I don't know about you fools," Angelo says, "but it's 12:30 and I'm starving. Are we ordering lunch or what?"

"I can grab it," I immediately offer, slipping right back into assistant mode. I suggest a nearby deli and they all agree. After getting their orders, I tell Vin I'll be back shortly.

I enjoy getting out of the office and doing errands, especially when it's a beautiful day out. Today, it's warm and sunny, so I put my sunglasses on, grab my purse which holds a company credit card, and head outside. My heels hit the pavement and warm sunshine touches my skin. It feels so good.

Even though we only just met, I decide that I really like Vin's brothers. They seem fun and flirty. I also like his younger sister a lot, too. It would be nice to have such a large family and my heart yearns for the kind of relationship they all seem to have. A close-knit group who can joke with each other or have a serious conversation. I can feel the way they support one another and I have a feeling they'd go down swinging and fighting til the death for each other.

I'm almost to the deli, completely absorbed in my thoughts and the beautiful day, when a car pulls up to the curb. Before I realize what's happening, a man grabs my arm and pushes me inside. Dropping down on the backseat, I'm about to scream when I find myself face to face with Caleb Durant. Instead, my skin crawls and fear washes over me, absolutely paralyzing my vocal cords.

"Hello, Hannah," Caleb says, his leering gaze dropping to where my blouse sags open, revealing the tops of my breasts. "That is your real name, right?"

I don't say a word to confirm or deny it. Instead, I quickly fix my shirt and toss him a cold glare. "Let me out," I demand. I hate that he knows my real name, but I suppose he could've easily found out from Dexter Creed.

"That's not a very nice greeting. Why don't you try that again? I'm sure you can be more polite."

"Let. Me. Out." I'm not playing games with this asshole.

"Fine. Be a bitch," he snaps. "Let's skip right over the pleasantries and get down to the nitty gritty."

"What're you talking about?" I ask, confused.

"I'm coming over later to pick you up for dinner."

"No thanks."

He chuckles. "It's more of a fact than an invitation, sweet Hannah. You see, I'm still annoyed about what happened at the White Auction. You should've been mine that night. But, Rossi had to swoop in and steal you from right under my nose. So, now you owe me an evening."

Is he crazy? I shake my head. "I don't owe you anything."

"See, we can do this the easy way or the hard way. It's really all up to you how we move forward."

"I'm not going to dinner with you."

"Fine, we'll do it the hard way." His face flushes with anger. "Last chance, Hannah. If you don't accept my offer then your life is going to get very difficult."

I press my lips together in answer, refusing to give in to this jerk.

His gaze ices over and his eyes narrow into slits. "Since you're being difficult, I'm now forced to play hardball. My first target will be Rossi Vineyard."

Shock fills me. Wait, what did he just say? "What?"

"That's right. I'm going to take it over."

"You can't do that!" I exclaim feeling the first waves of panic. *Can he?* How is that even possible? Rossi Vineyard belongs to Vin and his family.

"Oh, I can and I will," he assures me smugly. "Especially since they have no idea how much of their stock I've bought up recently."

Oh, no. My stomach sinks. "Please, don't," I plead. This is all my fault. If I hadn't inadvertently caught Caleb's attention at the auction then none of this would be happening right now. Vin and his family shouldn't lose something so important to them because of me.

"Agree to go to dinner with me tonight. And maybe I'll think about reconsidering my takeover. No promises, though," he adds pleasantly.

The idea that Vin and his family could lose one of their most important companies because of me makes me feel sick. I'm so upset, but what choice do I have? I don't have any option except to say yes and prevent this from happening. "Okay," I finally mumble, not happy in the least.

"Good. I'll pick you up after work. Five o'clock?"

I nod miserably.

"Look for the BMW." He winks at me and I throw up a little in my mouth. "See you soon, Hannah dear."

Ugh. I open the door and slip back out. If Vin loses Rossi Vineyard because of me, he'll never forgive me. There's nothing else I could've done. Nothing except agree to the dinner date to protect the Rossi family and their interests. To protect Vin.

Pulling my shoulders back, I continue down to the deli and wonder how in the hell I'm going to get through dinner with Caleb Durant. Even worse, what if he begins demanding more from me? How can I say no, but also make sure Vin, his family and their company remain safe?

I truly have no idea.

14

VIN

The moment Hannah returns from the deli with lunch, I can tell something is wrong. She's withdrawn, quiet and uncommunicative. She's just not her usual cheerful self and I wonder why. Is it because of what happened between us earlier? Does she regret it? I hope not because as much as I'm trying to keep the physical stuff separate from the emotional crap, it hurts me to see her upset.

You can't fall for her, I tell myself. *You absolutely cannot lose your heart to another woman.*

Not after what happened the last time.

After my brothers leave, Hannah and I start to work on a new project together, and the scorching heat between us earlier that nearly set us on fire is completely gone. It's as though her mind is a million miles away.

At one point, I flat-out ask her what's wrong. She shrugs my question off, says nothing and changes the subject. But, I can read her too well. Something is definitely bothering her and I vow to find out what.

I quickly find out that Hannah is stubborn as hell when she wants to be. She clams up and closes off, making it clear that the conversation is over. *Maybe for now,* I reluctantly concede, but I will find out what's going on in that pretty, little head of hers.

The rest of the day flies by because we're so busy and I realize how much I love working with Hannah. Having her by my side, listening to her opinions and suggestions is exciting because she has such a fresh, original and youthful outlook. She's also passionate about the brand and her job. And, God help me, I'm passionate about her.

I want her so damn badly. On a deep, primitive level that's starting to make me a little—okay, a lot—crazy for her. So nuts, in fact, that after she says a quick goodbye and races out the door, I follow her.

I have never followed a woman before in my life.

But, I'm extremely concerned and suspicious about her sudden mood swing when she returned with lunch. Her normally cheerful demeanor had completely evaporated. Something had happened while she was out and, dammit, I'm going to find out what.

And if I have to kick someone's ass, I will. Because nobody is allowed to upset my angel like that. Fucking no one.

Keeping my distance and making sure to stay out of view, I follow her down to the lobby, watch her walk outside and head straight over to a BMW. Squinting, I try to see through the glass and get a glimpse of the driver, but the windows are tinted and the car is parked at an angle. I can't make out shit other than it's a flashy, red sports model.

No thanks. I much prefer my Mercedes to that "hey, look at me" car. *Pathetic.*

When Hannah pulls the door open and gets inside, my heart freezes up because I get a glimpse of the driver. Fucking Caleb Durant. It takes every ounce of my self-control not to storm over there and yank Hannah back out of that car.

My heart sinks. Why is she going with him? What don't I know? What kind of game is she playing? Why in the hell would she willingly go with that asshole? My hands clench into fists and I bite down so hard, I'm surprised that I don't crack a tooth. Immediately, my first response is anger; then, my fractured heart fills so heavy with doubts that it sinks like a brick in my chest.

I've been cheated on before and it's what damaged me so thoroughly that I've avoided serious relationships for years. Cynda fucking broke me. Now, seeing Hannah go off with another man infuses me with jealousy, confusion and fury.

But, after a minute, I begin to think more logically. She called me half-scared to death after her last run-in with Durant. Why would she not be afraid of him now? What the hell is going on? And, above all, why didn't she confide in me if something is going on?

As the car pulls away from the curb, I bolt outside and head straight to my Mercedes. Luckily, it's still parked at the curb where Enzo dropped it off earlier after borrowing it. His car is in the shop and after our lunch, he needed to run an errand. Like the good brother I am, I said okay. Of course, in typical Enzo fashion, he left it out front with the valet who said I'd get it later. That was hours ago. Luckily, the valet isn't going to allow the president's car to be towed.

Pulling out into traffic, I keep my eyes on the BMW. The bright red car stands out in traffic, so it's easy to spot, and I make my way closer, weaving in and out of the other cars, taxis and buses. It's rush hour, so the streets are jam-packed and I pay close attention to where Durant is taking Hannah.

Taking *my* Hannah.

The idea of them together makes me sick. Something has to be going on. But what? Determined to figure it out, I follow them all the way to Valentino's, some swank, little restaurant near the docks. While Durant pulls up to the valet, I park illegally and wait, growing more pissed with every passing second. Something isn't adding up. Maybe I should just walk away, but the protector in me needs to know that Hannah is alright. When she gets out of the car, there's no missing the miserable look on her face. She doesn't want to be there and my wobbly heart steadies.

And, if she doesn't want to be here then I'm going in to rescue her. Even if I have to plow through Caleb Durant and forcefully remove Hannah from the situation. I don't give a fuck. Right now I'm feeling edgy and supremely pissed off. No one—and I mean fucking no one— takes my angel away from me and makes her do something she doesn't want to do.

Flashbacks from the White Auction fill my head and I remember how Durant looked at Hannah that night. Like he wanted to fuck every orifice of her body and then swallow her whole. It makes me sick.

Once they're inside, I pull up to the valet, get out and hand the guy a crisp one-hundred dollar bill. "Watch my car. I won't be long."

He pockets the money fast. "Sure thing, sir."

With a nod, I march up the steps and, right before I enter the restaurant, doubts punch me in the gut and heart. What if they're on a date? What if I just imagined she looked miserable? What if the jealousy burning through my veins right now is making me lose my damn mind?

It's hard for me to draw in a breath much less think clearly and I storm by the hostess podium and scan the restaurant. The lighting is dim and the atmosphere is romantic Which, of course, only angers me further. By the time I see them sitting beside each other at a corner table, my blood pressure is skyrocketing and everything in my vision is a hazy red.

Not thinking clearly, fueled by rage, I stalk up to their table. "What the fuck is going on here?" I demand. I don't even try to keep my voice low or mask my anger. It's already hit the boiling point and there's no holding back. Pretending to be civil is beyond me and, at this point, impossible. I'm fucking livid.

Caleb's eyes go wide then narrow into tiny slits while Hannah blows out a breath that can only be described as relief. She also looks shocked as hell to see me.

"Not that it's any of your damn business, Rossi, but Hannah and I are on a date," Caleb states in a superior tone that makes me want to punch him in the face.

I turn my attention to Hannha. "Is this true?" I ask.

Her face pales at my question and she's fumbling with the napkin on the table. When she doesn't answer me right away, my suspicions return. This morning my fingers were knuckle-deep inside her pussy as I made her come hard on the conference room table. And now she's out on a date with this scum? Nothing is adding up and my head is spinning.

Why isn't she answering me? Why isn't she begging me to take her far away from this asshole? I don't understand what's going on. All I know is I'm not about to let these two finish their so-called date.

It's fucking over.

"C'mon, Hannah. We're leaving."

"No, Rossi, she's not," Caleb says in a low, smug voice.

Again, she hesitates and my heart twists in my chest. Why isn't she jumping across the table and leaping into my arms?

"Yeah, she is," I state firmly, "and if you try to stop her, I'm going to kick your fucking ass all over this restaurant."

"You wouldn't dare." The bastard leans back in his seat, drapes his arm across the back of Hannah's chair and has the audacity to smile at me. Durant is so sure of himself, so damn cocky, and I've had enough.

Then he really pushes me over the edge when he says, "Make yourself scarce, Rossi. The lady isn't interested."

All of my anger focuses on Durant and I reach across the table, grab him by the lapels of his suit and drag him forward. Dishes and glasses clatter to the floor and Hannah gasps, jumping up and out of the way. I pull my fist back and slam it into his face. Durant goes flying backwards, hits the wall and drops like a sack of potatoes.

But, he doesn't stay down. Instead, he jumps back up and charges, hitting me in a low tackle in the knees, and knocking me flat on my ass. We roll around, throwing punches, and I can hear the diners around us getting upset.

But, I don't stop. I can't. It's like something possesses me and all I can do is fight. Durant is surprisingly strong and he gives as good as he gets. I manage to get some well-placed hits in, but so does he. Eventually, someone yanks me backwards, away from Durant. At the same time, a waiter is pulling him off me, too.

Now that we've been broken apart, I'm done. Getting out of here is my first priority and I shrug off the man holding my arm, stalk forward and wrap my fingers around Hannah's upper arm, pulling her toward the exit. I pass the manager who I know and grunt, "Send me a bill for any damage."

Once we're outside, I practically drag Hannah over to my car, open the door and push her inside. Then I walk around, get in and squeal away from the curb. I need my anger to die down before I ask her for an explanation. Hannah, on the other hand, is ready to talk. And, to my utter surprise, she blasts me.

"What is wrong with you?" she exclaims, turning to face me in her seat. "Do you have any idea what kind of scene you just caused?"

I shrug a dismissive shoulder, not caring in the least.

"Someone could've been hurt or worse," she scolds me.

I try to reel my temper in, but my fingers tighten around the steering wheel and, for the first time, I notice my bloody knuckles. My cheekbone hurts, too, and I glance in the rear view mirror to see it already looks like it's swelling and bruised. *Fucker.* Seeing that just makes me madder. Hannah is still talking, but I've tuned her out. That is until I hear her say, "I'm not yours!"

That one statement pulls me back into the argument I was trying to avoid. I really didn't want to say something I might later regret, but it's too late now. Beyond pissed, I spin the wheel and turn the car into a nearby alley. I shouldn't be driving while I'm feeling this emotional and upset, anyway. Slamming the car into park, I turn my full attention to Hannah.

"What're you saying? Your his? You belong to him?" I seethe.

"What? No!"

I throw my hands up in absolute frustration. "You're driving me so goddamn crazy I can't think straight!"

"You don't understand," she tells me.

"Tell me then, Hannah. What don't I understand? Because all I know is you didn't look like you wanted to leave him."

"Of course, I did!" she shouts. "But…I couldn't."

"That doesn't make any goddamn sense!"

"Neither do you! One minute you're hot and the next you're cold. I can't read you, I don't know what you want from me anymore. You want sex and then push me away and turn cool," she accuses.

My eyes narrow and I'm one step away from showing her exactly what I want.

"Maybe you're just playing games. Or, I'm imagining things and whatever happened between us…." Her voice trails off. "It didn't mean anything. All I know is I don't belong to you any more than I belong to Caleb Durant."

That does it. I grab her arm, pulling her closer. "If I remember correctly, *your* blood was on *my* sheets. Or have you forgotten?"

Her blue eyes widen in shock then narrow. "You're such a jerk."

"You're *mine*, Hannah," I growl, yanking her onto my lap. "Whether you like it or not."

The last of my control snaps and I slam my mouth against hers, claiming her. She makes a frustrated sound before melting against me. The kiss is wild, out of control and feral. I'm marking her as mine and making sure she knows it. My patience is long gone and all I know is I am desperate for her. Dying to sink inside her hot, wet pussy and take what's mine. What's always been mine since the night she gave me her virginity.

Scorching need drives us together and she's writhing against me. There isn't much room to maneuver, but I shove the seat back to give us a couple of more inches. Grabbing her skirt, I yank it up to her waist and rip her silky panties right off, tossing them into the back-seat. Hannah gasps then makes a sexy mewling sound as I release my rigid cock. She grinds against me and my hips slam up, sinking deep into her soaking wet pussy.

We both let out a long groan then she begins to move, drawing me deeper, as I pump into her. Our mating is out of control and fierce. I've never had sex like this before. I have zero control over my body, over my emotions, over what's happening between us. All I can do is thrust into her, desperate to be one with her.

I yank my mouth free from hers and suck in a deep, shaky breath. My fingers drop, find her clit and begin massaging hard. "Say you're mine, Hannah," I hiss, pumping furiously, bouncing her up and down on my lap. "Tell me."

"Oh, God!" She squeezes my dick hard and has it in a chokehold as she rides me. "Vin…"

"Say it!" I order, my voice a harsh rasp.

"I'm yours!"

"Fuck yes, you are." I increase the pressure on her swollen clit and she arches back against the steering wheel, hitting the horn. We both ignore the beep, though, as our orgasms come crashing down around us, propelling us into pure, radiant bliss. "And don't you fucking forget it."

My entire frame shudders hard and my release empties into her tight, little body. It belatedly occurs to me that we just had wild, unprotected sex, but I can't think too hard about that right now. My cock is still spurting deep inside her core and I dig my fingers into her fleshy ass, my hips still pumping.

Fuck.

I think I'm falling in love with Hannah and that scares the shit out of me. Because it can't happen. I won't let it. Despite what my stupid heart wants.

15

HANNAH

I scream out Vin's name, my inner muscles tightening around his hard length, and then we orgasm at the exact same moment. Dropping forward, I melt against him, breathing hard. Too late, I realize we didn't use protection. Maybe I should be feeling some sort of regret, but...I'm not. Instead, I find myself still spasming around his cock, caught in a maelstrom of pure bliss, and so turned on by the fact he's inside me bare that my body unexpectedly jolts with another orgasm.

Crying out, I stiffen in his arms and come again. I've heard of multiple orgasms, but never really understood the term until this moment. Trembling hard, lost in sensation, I bury my face against his chest and want to weep.

I love being with Vin. Our relationship is wild, free and unpredictable. But he isn't giving himself to me fully and his walls are still so high. I'm not sure what I can do to get past them.

When he lifts me up and off, I slide back over into the passenger seat, pulling my skirt back down. Neither of us says anything for a long moment. Then Vin adjusts his seat and starts the car.

I wait and wait for him to say something...anything...but he just stares straight ahead, eyes glued to the road, fingers gripping the steering wheel in a death hold.

What is he thinking? Why won't he communicate with me? Yet, I suppose that I can say the same thing about myself. I can't seem to force a word out and I'm suddenly so sad because I think it's pretty clear that I want him so much more than he wants me.

"Take me home. Please," I finally whisper. He isn't giving me the reassurance I need or telling me he cares. I'm questioning everything and I feel hot tears threaten. God, when did I become such an emotional wreck? I guess falling hard for a man does that to a girl. Especially after I've given him my everything and he's giving me nothing in return. Not emotionally, anyway.

Vin is my hero and my protector, but he gets super close and then pulls away. Every time. It's mentally exhausting and I don't know what he wants from me. Other than a fast fuck in his office or car. And that makes me sad because I want so much more. I know we have the potential to be so damn good together. Why can't he see that? Why won't he take a chance and leap with me?

Glancing over, I study him and wonder what he's afraid of? His handsome face is set in hard lines and angles, and he's glaring at the road ahead. A part of me is ashamed that I gave in to him so easily just now, but there's no use fighting the overpowering connection constantly trying to pull us together. We're like two magnets, constantly drawn to each other. Fighting the pull is useless.

Even though I want to talk about what's happening between us, I press my lips together and remain quiet until we reach my apartment building. But the urge to discuss our relationship overwhelms me. I have to know where Vin's head is at. Does he care about me at all? Or am I just a conquest? A little girl to be toyed with until he grows bored?

Vin puts the car in park and stares out the windshield, looking slightly wrecked and confused. As though he can't quite grasp what's happening either.

"Vin? Can we talk?"

"Okay," he says slowly. His attention finally turns to me and my heart catches. He's so damn handsome and I reach over and wipe my lipstick off his face.

I think it's time to take a leap of faith and ask what he wants. Just be blunt and forthright. Once I know where he stands with me, with *us*, we can either move forward together or separately. Although the latter hurts so badly, I don't want to even think about it.

"What's going on?" I ask quietly.

"What do you mean?"

"Between us?" I clarify even though he knows damn well what I mean. "One minute you're hot and the next—" I gesture between us, "—you're cold. Am I just a game to you? Another notch on your bedpost? Or, do you see a potential future with us?"

There. I said it. Bracing myself for his answer, I hold my breath and stare into his amazing green eyes. And, instead of answering my question, he glances out the window again.

"This isn't a very good neighborhood," he murmurs. "You should move somewhere safer."

I merely blink, confused by how he's trying to avoid my very serious question. Then, I get annoyed. "That's not what I asked," I state, my voice turning cool and full of aggravation. "Besides, it's really none of your business where I live."

He focuses back on me, green eyes narrowing slightly. Finally, I get a reaction from him.

"It is, though," he insists. "I want you safe."

I let out a frustrated breath. "Honestly, Vin, why do you even care?"

"What's that supposed to mean?"

"I ask you something and you completely ignore me."

"I'm not ignoring you, Hannah. I hear every word you say. Every comma. But…" He swipes a hand down his face. "I'm not the man for you."

Confusion sweeps through me. "Why would you even say that? You're amazing, Vin, and—"

"I don't do serious relationships, Hannah," he says, cutting me off. "I can't give you what you want."

My heart sinks. "How do you know what I want?"

"You deserve a man who can give you forever—"

"I'm not asking for forever! I just want to spend time with you and keep getting to know you better. You can't deny how good we are together, Vin, so don't even try."

His lips remain tightly pressed together and he knows I'm right, so he doesn't even try to deny it.

Feeling a surge of confidence, I press forward. "What do you want from me, Vin? An employee or a girlfriend?"

When he doesn't say anything, merely shakes his head sadly, I have my answer. White-hot anger pours through me, but, really, I have no one to blame but myself. Vin has been nothing but honest and upfront with me from the beginning. I'm the one who chose to give him my virginity. He's made me no promises which means he's broken none, either.

Throwing the car door open, I hop out and slam it shut. The earlier sunshine is gone and the sky is dark with the threat of an approaching storm. It matches my mood perfectly and I do my best to hold back the tears until I get inside. So he can't see me or how upset I am.

The moment I step into my building, the tears start streaming down my face in a torrent. Sobs tear from my throat as I rush up the stairs, unable to see anything in front of me. It's just all a blur and I make the stupid mistake of running straight into Liza Dixon, my nosy neighbor.

"Hannah! Are you okay? What's wrong, dear?" she asks.

Even though I always stop and talk to Liza, I can't right now. I'm too upset and I hurry past, my head down and head straight for my door. The key shakes in my hand and it takes me a few times to get it open. Once I'm inside, I quickly shut and lock it then turn around, lean back and slide down to the floor.

Overwhelming emotion and a fresh onslaught of tears pour from my already-puffy eyes. Damn Vincentius Rossi. Damn Dexter Creed. And, most of all, damn me for falling head over heels for a man who doesn't want me.

It hurts and I press a hand over my heart. I truly thought we had something special, but he refuses to acknowledge it. Why does he say he can't give me what I want? What is he so afraid of? If he felt anything toward me, wouldn't it make sense that he'd want to try? That he'd want to be with me, too?

I'm not sure how long I sit on the floor. I guess until I'm all cried out. Eventually, I drag myself up and head into the bathroom. I turn on the shower, unbutton my blouse, shimmy my skirt off and freeze when I realize that my panties are still in the backseat of Vin's car.

"Oh, God," I groan and slide a hand down my face. Could this day get any more worse? As if in answer, there's a knock on my door. My heart jumps up into my throat and the first thing I think is it's Vin. Grabbing my bathrobe off the back of the door, I slip it on and hurry to the door. Pulling it open, I frown at the delivery man standing there and holding a huge vase of blood red roses.

What in the world?

"Hannah Everson?" he asks.

"Uh, yeah."

"I have a delivery for you."

He hands it over and the vase is heavy and weighs a ton. "Do I, ah, owe you anything?" I ask, not sure of the protocol since no one has ever sent me flowers before. "A tip or—"

"Everything has been taken care of. Just need a signature."

"Oh, okay, hang on." I turn and set the flowers down on the table and then scrawl a quick signature on his ipad.

"All set. Have a good day."

"You, too," I respond and slowly shut the door. I'm beyond confused. Looking for an answer, I walk over to the vase and pluck the card out. Hoping they're from Vin, but knowing that's impossible since I just left him, I unseal the envelope and frown.

Dearest Hannah, I won't hold you responsible for what happened tonight. This is all Rossi's fault and he will pay. You still owe me dinner, though, and I shall collect, sweet girl. Apologies for what happened and I will make it up to you. I promise. Looking forward to the next time, Caleb.

"Ughhh," I groan and drop the card. I don't want his stupid roses and I certainly never want to see Caleb Durant again. I hear a distant buzzing and walk over to my purse. Pulling out my phone, I check the caller ID, but it's flashing "unknown." A part of me is tempted to answer, but I don't and, instead, I let it drop into voicemail. A moment later, there's a beep signaling a new message.

After hitting a couple of buttons, I lift the phone to my ear and listen. And, of course, it's the last person on the planet who I want to be hearing from.

"Hello, Hannah, it's Caleb. I hope you received the roses okay. Their beauty pales in comparison to yours—" I roll my eyes, "—but, a man can try. My apologies that things got out of hand and our dinner was ruined. Rossi is a loose cannon who will have to be dealt with. Clearly.

But don't worry your pretty little head about that. I'll call you later so we can reschedule our dinner. I have a feeling once we're able to spend more time together, you'll get to like me even more. I tend to grow on people."

Yeah, just like a wart, I think.

"Have a good night and we'll talk soon. *Ciao.*"

A shiver runs down my spine when I think about meeting Caleb again. But, really what choice do I have? He's threatening to take over Rossi Vineyard and I can't let that happen. Plus, his comment about Vin being a loose cannon who will have to be dealt with leaves me more upset than I was before.

Should I warn Vin? I let out a sigh and realize Vin can take care of himself. I'm the last person he wants to see or hear from. Which leads me to my next dilemma—should I quit the only job I've ever enjoyed. A job that I'm good at and like waking up in the morning to go to? A job that pays me an obscene amount of money and provides me with endless perks?

Because the truth is I can't handle working so closely with Vin every day. It hurts too much.

Instead of heading back to the bathroom to take a shower, I wander into my tiny kitchen and pluck a bottle of wine out of the cupboard. Of course, it's a fancy bottle from Rossi Vineyard that Vin gave me to try. At this point, I couldn't care less about how it tastes. I just need some alcohol to take the edge off and dull my senses. Ideally, I'll get stinking drunk and pass out before I start crying again.

Because the worst thing in the world has happened to me. I've fallen in love with an emotionally-unavailable man. Sure, he's given me his body—several times—but he keeps his heart locked up tight and far out of my reach.

Why, dammit? What happened in his past to make him so closed off? I wonder.

I wish I had an answer, but I don't. Vin never told me anything about his past or any previous relationships he'd had. But I have a good feeling that the answer lies there. Most likely, some uncaring woman fucked him over and, as a result, he shut himself down and doesn't allow himself to become emotionally-invested or serious. It's a tale as old as time, right?

And that's a damn shame because Vincentius Rossi would make the most amazing boyfriend or husband. He's caring, considerate, protective and an amazing lover. I don't think he even realizes how wonderful he is and that makes me sad. It's more than a damn shame. It's a tragedy.

But what can I do?

After fighting with the cork, I pour myself a big glass of dark red deliciousness and take a long sip, praying for sweet oblivion to come fast. Three glasses later, after curling up on my couch and crying some more, I finally fall asleep.

And, of course, all of my wine-induced dreams are filled with Vin's handsome face.

16

VIN

It's official. I am the world's biggest jerk. A completely selfish asshole who just crushed the sweetest woman's heart.

After losing all self-control, causing a scene at the restaurant and then fucking Hannah in the car, I tell her I don't do relationships or forever. Even though I know that's exactly what she wants.

"Am I just a game to you? Another notch on your bedpost? Or, do you see a potential future with us?"

Her words still sting but the answer to all of those questions is—has to be—no. I can't give her what she wants or needs. Being vulnerable once before nearly destroyed me. I refuse to do it again despite hurting us both in the process. At this point, I'm in self-preservation mode.

And, yeah, I am a stubborn fuck. So despite how much this hurts, I'm not changing my mind.

Pinching the bridge of my nose, I skip past my endless wine collection and go straight to the top-shelf whiskey. Tonight, I plan to get stinking drunk and I'm going to drink until I stop feeling so awful. I fully plan to pass out on my couch and wish that I'd never crossed paths with Hannah Everson.

No, that's not completely accurate. Because if I hadn't won her at that auction, she would've been at Caleb Durant's mercy. And, I don't think that ruthless sonofabitch possesses an ounce of mercy. Hannah is too sweet to be left to his devices.

Which has me wondering all over again why she went out to dinner with him tonight. I never did get an answer. She clearly didn't want to be there with him, she looked utterly relieved when I showed up, yet she'd merely said I wouldn't understand.

Dropping onto my couch, I kick my shoes off then wrestle out of my suit jacket. My hand wraps around the glass of whiskey and I take a nice, long soothing sip. I think I've managed to screw everything up so royally between Hannah and I that it's officially over.

Suddenly, I sit up straighter and curse. What if she quits? Would she do that? Not come back to a job she likes and is good at because of me?

"Fuck," I hiss. I suppose it won't be a surprise if I receive a resignation letter from her. And that pisses me off all over again. But, I'm not angry at her. I'm angry at myself for being such a complete idiot and handling everything wrong.

I really couldn't have done a worse job, I think and take another drink.

"You really suck," I tell myself. "On an epic level."

I don't want to see or talk to anyone, so I turn my phone off and focus all of my attention on feeling sorry for myself. If Hannah doesn't return to the office, what can I do? Hunt her down and force her to work for me? No, that's not an option. Although, it is tempting.

God. I shake my head then lean it back and close my eyes as I ponder what a complete madman I've become since the night Hannah walked into my life. I've always had iron self-control and a logical thought process. But with Hannah, that all goes up in a puff of smoke. She makes me crazy with the need to protect her. I want to make sure she's okay at all times and I don't care what rules I have to break or who I need to beat up to make sure she's cared for.

Speaking of which…

I run my fingers over my face and flinch slightly. That bastard Durant got a few good punches in and there will be bruises tomorrow. Pulling up the edge of my shirt, I look down at my aching side and cringe. Yep, it already looks black and blue.

"Fucker," I grumble, drop my shirt back in place and take a long drink of whiskey. The alcohol will dull the pain soon. And, eventually, I'll pass out and forget all about the absolute shit show that today turned out to be.

And tomorrow you'll remember it all over again, I remind myself. Maybe, but for now, I'm done. Time to drink until I can't feel any longer. Until I'm in a drunken stupor where I'm not caring anymore.

Because that's the problem. Hannah is making me feel things that I haven't felt since Cynda. I keep comparing the two. I can't help it. After meeting Cynda Drake, I fell hard and fast. And, I thought she had too. That was my first mistake—believing that bitch had actual feelings.

With hindsight, I was young and stupidly hung up on her because I thought she was beautiful and her family was powerful. She wasn't even half as lovely as Hannah, though. Cynda's beauty was cool and distant. There was an icy quality about her that I chose to ignore and, instead, I focused on how hot we were between the sheets.

It didn't last, though. Cynda grew bored and went elsewhere to find a new thrill. Someone new to conquer. When I walked in on her fucking an acquaintance of mine in the coat room closet of a fundraiser we were attending, I couldn't believe what I was seeing. My supposed woman propped against the wall with her legs wrapped around another man's waist, moaning and writhing as he thrusted into her. At that point, we were engaged.

I remember the way her left hand hung over his shoulder and how with each thrust, it jerked and the diamond engagement ring on her finger caught the light just right and glinted.

Bang, glint. Bang, glint. Bang, glint.

I'm not sure how long I stood there, rooted in place, watching my fiancée getting the shit pounded out of her. Eventually, her gaze caught mine and instead of gasping or stopping or, hell, showing any kind of remorse, she smiled.

She fucking smiled at me with another man's dick inside of her. And then she came in his arms, shuddering and grinning at me. I remember turning around, feeling dazed, and I stalked into the nearest men's room where I walked into a stall and hurled up my dinner.

Cynda Drake's betrayal left me wrecked. That moment of walking in on her in the middle of having sex with another man broke something inside of me and it hasn't been the same since. I'd thought I loved her and believed she loved me back. I truly thought we were going to spend our lives together. I should've known better and, with hindsight, there were signs. Signs I chose to ignore because I wanted to believe in her—in us—so badly. I wanted to trust her even when she would often disappear. Or, when she'd turn up much later with her hair askew and makeup slightly mussed.

Deep down, I'd had my suspicions, but I'd turned a blind eye. So damn stupid. I think she wanted me to find out about her infidelity and to confront her. She thrived on drama and power. And, I'm sure, there were quite a few infidelities, but I only knew about the one. It was all I could handle at the time, anyway.

I immediately broke off our engagement and moved out of the loft we'd been sharing. She didn't seem all that heartbroken about it and had told me to get over myself. Then she'd asked me if I had really expected her to only have sex with one man for the rest of her life.

"Hell, we're not even married yet and you're already acting like a ball and chain," she'd joked.

She'd continued to demasculinize me in every way possible, telling me how I'd never been able to fully satisfy her. All her barbed words hurt and I took them far too personally. But how could I not?

After walking away that night, I broke into a million little pieces. I locked myself up in my old apartment, refusing to see or talk to anyone, and I mourned the loss of our relationship. Or, the idea of what I thought our relationship had been. Over time, I put myself back together, but it was a process and I'd promised myself that I would never open my heart to another woman again.

It just wasn't fucking worth it.

Ignoring my glass, I reach for the whiskey and take a swig straight out of the bottle. *Cynda hadn't been worth it*, a little voice says, *but maybe Hannah is different. Maybe she's worth the risk.*

Squeezing my eyes closed, I shut that dangerous thought down fast and continue to drink myself into a stupor. But even drunk, I dream about my *Angioletto*.

The next day I'm more hungover than I ever remember being in my life. After swallowing down a handful of aspirin and taking a quick shower, I get dressed. Very slowly because my entire body aches and my head pounds like there's a marching band in it. From the fight with Caleb to the bottle of whiskey I demolished, I physically feel like shit.

I'd almost forgotten my brothers and I have a meeting with the Five Families today. Normally, I don't go to these, but since things have changed, Miceli expects my presence and support.

Luckily, the meeting isn't until noon and by that time I'm feeling a smidge better. At least like a human being again. I drive over to the secure location which changes constantly. This time, the five most powerful families in the city meet in an Italian restaurant that's currently closed to the public. When I walk in, the scent of garlic bread and spicy tomato sauce hits my nose, and I lay a hand over my stomach, telling myself to hold it together and not retch all over the floor.

It's going to be a while until I touch whiskey again. Hell, until I eat or drink anything again.

There's a large, round table set with plates and it looks like we're getting lunch. No thanks. My vicious hangover has cured me of any desire for food. At least, for the moment. My brothers and Carlotta are already seated and I pull out a chair between Miceli and Enzo and sit down.

"You look like shit," Miceli states.

"Worse than shit," Enzo adds.

"Gee, thanks." I grumble and touch my temple. A headache is throbbing and it feels like a toy soldier is in my head, banging his drum against my skull over and over, alongside the damn marching band that's still playing.

"Are you hungover?" Angelo asks with a smirk.

Carlotta, sitting on his opposite side, leans around him to look at me, nosy as ever. "What happened to you?"

"I almost drank myself to death last night, if it's anyone's business," I whisper-hiss.

"You're an idiot," Miceli says in a low voice, and I sink down into my chair and cross my arms, not in the mood to hear everyone start bitching. Because it's inevitable and happens in every meeting I've attended so far.

Once everyone appears situated, Miceli welcomes them and starts the meeting. My brother is a take charge kind of guy and runs this city smoothly and fairly, but with an iron fist. He doesn't tolerate bullshit and if someone is causing trouble, they tend to disappear.

"It's been brought to my attention that Caleb Durant is threatening to move in on Rossi territory, specifically my family's wine company. Does anyone have any specific details for us?"

What? I slowly sit up straighter in my chair and listen as the others offer any intel they have. There's only one reason Durant would target our most successful business.

"It's because of me and Hannah," I say under my breath.

"Explain, please," Miceli says, and it's not a request.

The representatives from the Bianchi's, the DeLuca's, the Caparelli's and the Milano's focus on me, as well as my own family. I clear my throat and say, "I outbid Durant at an auction and he hasn't taken it well."

"Auction?" old man Caparelli echoes, sounding confused. "He wants to destroy you over losing a piece of art?"

"She's definitely a piece of art," I murmur. "Her name is Hannah and he's obsessed with her. He's also pissed that he lost out on winning her virginity."

"Ahh, the White Auction."

I didn't want to get into details about why I spent over one-hundred grand on her and how nothing happened that night. It's none of their business.

"Anyway, we, ah, started spending more time together and I hired her to work at Rossi Vineyard. Apparently, Durant didn't like that. He started following Hannah and she'd get upset and call me." Well, until that last time. She didn't call and, instead, willingly got right into

Durant's car and went to dinner with him. My already unsteady gut churns.

"It makes sense," Milano says. "Caleb has always been a vengeful fuck who doesn't deal well with rejection."

"He's always been jealous of us and our control," Aldo DeLucca, Alessia's father, adds. "Personally, I don't do business with him and I never will. He's an arrogant prick who can't be trusted."

"So we make sure he's no longer a threat. To any of us." Miceli looks out over the others. "We start by destroying his business."

"And if that doesn't work?" Gabriella Bianche asks. She's a feisty one. Cousins to Rocco Bianche who Micelli killed after he'd kidnapped Alessia.

"It'll work," Enzo responds. The two of them stare at each other a moment too long and I wonder if I'm the only one who notices the tension there. *Hmm, very interesting.* I'm going to have to ask my little brother how he feels about the lovely Ms. Bianche.

"Then we take him out permanently," Miceli states, interrupting my thoughts. "Anyone have an issue with that?"

No one says a word.

"Good."

Until recently, I've stayed out of the meetings and political BS when it comes to the Five Families. I know what we all do, what we're capable of doing, yet I've kept my distance and ignorance. But sitting here now, seeing how things are handled and how they get done sends a chill down my spine. Honestly, I've never been happier to be the second-born son. If I have my way, I'll focus on running our legit business, Rossi Vineyard, and leave the "permanent" stuff to the others. I was never meant to be a mafia leader and I'm quite content that role fell to Miceli.

The ruling families are more bloodthirsty than I knew and they would never let an enemy usurp even a fraction of their power or hold on the city. And, though I normally don't feel the need to defend my territory or fully embrace the breadth and depth of the mafia power my family holds, I remember the rage I felt at the restaurant earlier. How I stormed up to Durant and wanted to kill him. Wanted to destroy him with my bare fists. He brings out my mafia blood, making it boil, and when I picture his smug face, I know I'm just as capable of doing the horrific things that everyone else in this room is, too.

If Caleb Durant touches one hair on Hannah's head, I will end him. Permanently and with zero remorse.

17

HANNAH

I'm not sure if I eventually passed out or just cried myself to sleep. Whatever the case, my dreams are filled with Vin and he's always just out of my reach, disappearing the moment I reach out to touch him.

At some point, morning comes and it's Saturday, so I tuck my knees up to my chest and don't worry about getting up or going to work. I'm still trying to decide if I can stay and work for Vin, but I don't see how that's going to be possible. It's just going to be too damn painful to face him every day. I don't think my heart can take it.

Drifting in and out of sleep, putting off getting up, I start having strange dreams about Caleb. I'm back on the auction platform and, this time, Vin doesn't come to my rescue. Caleb ends up winning me and as he's dragging me out, I scream for Vin.

Jumping up from the nightmare, my eyes pop open and I breathe a sigh of relief. It isn't real, just a dream. Suddenly, a loud banging fills the air. Or, maybe someone's been banging for a couple of minutes now. I'm still fuzzy from sleep so I'm not sure.

"Hang on, I'm coming," I grumble, shoving my sleep-mussed hair back. Everything sways when I stand up and I give myself a moment to get steadied. Pain throbs through my head from drinking too much and my bleary eyes take a moment to adjust.

When I finally reach the door, I hear a woman saying my name. *Who is here so early?* I wonder and pull the door open. My gaze lands on Carlotta and there's a beautiful woman with long, dark hair standing beside her.

"Carlotta? What're you doing here?"

"We've come to mediate," Carlotta announces, walking past me. "Hannah, this is Alessia, Miceli's wife."

"Um, hi," I say, watching as they stroll into my dark apartment and begin opening the blinds and windows.

"Ugh, you need some fresh air in here," Carlotta states, wrinkling her nose. "It smells like a winery."

"That's being polite," Alessia says. "More like a brewery."

They eye the empty wine bottle still sitting on the coffee table.

"One bottle isn't that bad," Carlotta comments. "I've drowned my sorrows in more than that before."

After clearing away the empty glass and bottle, they fluff the pillows on my couch and sit down. Looks like this is going to turn into an interrogation whether I like it or not.

"Can I wash up first?" I ask, looking from one woman to the other. My teeth have a layer of scum on them and my face feels crusty from all the salty tears I cried.

"Please," Carlotta says, plucking a bottle of electrolyte water from her large handbag. "You need to hydrate, too."

I nod, not knowing what to say, and head into the bathroom. I'm not sure whether I should be annoyed that they're here and prying, or if I think it's the sweetest, most caring thing anyone has ever done.

After putting myself into a semblance of order, I go back out into the living room and sit in the small armchair across from them. After cracking the bottle of water, I take a long swig then look at the women.

"We heard what's going on with Caleb Durant and how he and Vin fought over you the other night," Carlotta says.

"Over me?" I echo and shake my head. "No, they just don't like each other..." My voice trails off weakly. The women arch perfectly-plucked brows.

"They both want you," Carlotta states.

"Caleb does, but Vin doesn't," I immediately state. "He's made it very clear that he doesn't do serious relationships and he can't give me what I want."

The women exchange a look. "Forget about them for a moment, Hannah." Alessia's voice drops as she asks softly, "What do *you* want?"

"Forever," I whisper, tears filling my eyes. "But, he doesn't want me."

"I don't believe that at all." Carlotta leans forward, dark eyes meeting mine. "My brother cares about you. A lot. More than—well, more than I've ever seen him care before."

I shake my head sadly. "No. Not really. I mean, he has the urge to protect me, but he doesn't want to be with me. Not long term, anyway."

"Hannah, it isn't my place to tell you this, but did Vin ever tell you about Cynda Drake?"

I frown, not recognizing the name. "No."

Carlotta lets out a breath, debating what to say. "She and my brother were engaged a long time ago and it ended badly. She really hurt him

159

and ever since then, he hasn't allowed himself to be emotionally vulnerable with women. At least, not until you."

I knew nothing about Vin being engaged or hurt. My heart instantly aches for him and I wonder what happened exactly.

"You should talk to him about it," Carlotta urges, "because I think his past is what's holding him back now. Because he really cares about you, Hannah."

Hearing her say all this reignites the flicker of hope in my heart. Could it be true? Does Vin really care about me, but he's being wary because his heart was broken before?

"This all hits so close to home," Alessia says. "My older sister Gia was hurt terribly by a man she loved. She'd allowed herself to become numb and only recently met someone who's been helping tear down her walls." The women exchange a grin. "Have you met Leo Amato?"

I shake my head. "No."

"Leo is Miceli's best friend and personal guard," Alessia explains. "He's as loyal as they come and he was shot trying to protect me."

"Oh, my God," I gasp.

"He's fine now," Carlotta adds quickly.

"But he and Gia really hit it off during his recovery. She fussed all over him and now they're inseparable. Which makes me so incredibly happy. It's been a long time since I've seen my sister so full of happiness," Alessia says, smiling from ear to ear.

"Leo looks pretty happy, too," Carlotta adds, and they both chuckle.

"The point of all this, though, is people can come back from being burned by an ex," Alessia states wisely. "All it takes is finding the right one to help them overcome their insecurities and show them that it's okay to take a risk and love again."

"And we think that's you," Carlotta says, giving me a smile.

"Me?" I wish I could agree with them, but my shaky heart just isn't convinced. "As much as I'd like that, I don't think Vin is on the same page. He told me he can't give me forever."

"Of course that's what he told you," Carlotta says, "but what does he know? He's just talking out of fear. You need to go to him, Hannah. Well, only if you love him, of course. Do you? Love my brother?"

My heart flip-flops in my chest at her softly-spoken question. "Yes," I whisper. "So much."

Both women squeal and pop up off the coach. They hurry over and we all hug. It feels good to have their support and tears sting the back of my eyes. A moment later, they're sliding down my face and I'm a mess all over again.

"Why're you crying?" Carlotta asks.

I swipe a hand over my drippy nose. "It's just..." I sniff. "It was always just me and my mom. After she passed away, I've been all alone. At least until Vin. And now...well, you two almost feel like sisters."

"Aww!" They pull me into another big hug.

"I'd love to be your sister," Carlotta says.

"Me, too," Alessia adds.

"I'd like that," I say softly.

"Okay, you love my brother, so go get him. Make his stubborn ass see that you're his perfect person and he doesn't need to be scared because you won't hurt him like Cynda did."

"I'll talk to him," I promise, "and do my best to make him see that I would never betray or hurt him in any way."

We end up talking a little longer and then the women give me another huge hug and finally leave, allowing me to get ready and go see Vin. But, I'm not quite ready yet. With all of their words swirling around in my head, I can't deny that I'm hopeful. But the fear that he will reject me again is still strong and worries me. Tremendously.

After a shower, I get dressed, apply some quick makeup and throw my hair up in a messy bun. I don't want to spend a long time on how I look because this is who I am, take me or leave me.

And, I sincerely hope Vin will take me as I am. Messy, unglamorous and unsophisticated me who will love him fiercely. Fiercely and forever.

When I can't put it off any longer, I grab my phone and purse, then head out. Once I reach the lobby, I'm not expecting to see Caleb striding into my building. Dammit, the lock is still broken on the front door allowing him to waltz right in like he owns the place.

"Hello, sweet Hannah," he says, eyeing me up and down. My skin crawls in response.

"What're you doing here?" I ask, beyond frustrated, immediately noticing the bruises on his face from Vin's well-aimed punches. Inwardly, I smile.

Outwardly, though, I'm pissed. Why won't he leave me alone? Can't he see I'm not interested? What's it going to take to get rid of him once and for all?

"I'm sorry about how the evening went the other night and I'd like to reschedule."

"No," I say in a firm tone. I'm tired of playing this man's games and I won't let him walk all over me and threaten to hurt the Rossi family. Carlotta and Alessia's visit reminds me to be strong and to stand up for myself. I have people in my corner now. I'm not alone any longer and I'm not going to allow this snake to manipulate me any further.

"We have a date to finish," he hisses, those dark eyes narrowing dangerously.

"I never wanted to go out with you. You blackmailed me, but no more. The Rossi family has my back." I stand up straighter, refusing to back down or give in to him. "I'm not afraid of you."

He reaches me quicker than I imagined possible, grabs my arm and twists it hard. I yelp, but he doesn't loosen his vicious hold. "You should be afraid, Hannah," he hisses in my ear, reminding me more than ever of a snake. "You should be very afraid."

I whimper when he squeezes hard then yanks me toward the door. While we're walking out, I try to twist away, but it's impossible. As the door shuts with finality behind me, I swear I get a glimpse of Liza Dixon, hovering in the stairwell, watching.

Or, maybe that was wishful thinking and I just imagined it.

"Why don't you leave me alone? Can't you see I don't want to be with you? I love another man."

Caleb abruptly stops walking and glares daggers at me. "That will change. You're going to be with me now."

"No!" I cry, pulling and fighting. In the scuffle, my phone goes flying out of my hand and hits the pavement hard. Caleb kicks it aside, sending it clattering into the bushes, and I pull harder, trying to wrench free. But he's too strong and I find myself shoved into his blasted BMW again. The locks immediately click and I curse under my breath. Oh, God, how do I always get manhandled into these situations? After Caleb slides into the driver's seat, starting the car, I send him a deadly glare.

"I don't understand why you're fighting to be with a man who doesn't want you, Hannah. Can you explain that to me?"

His words sting and I press my lips together. Maybe that's true. But, I love Vin and after talking to his sister and Alessia, I can't give up on him. On us. At least not before telling him how I feel. Because, yeah, I'm ready to fight for our love.

As we drive away, to God only knows where, Caleb says, "I want access to Vin's computer files and I know you can get me in his system."

Alarm bells start clanging in my head. This is why Caleb is so determined to have me. It's not really me he wants, it's my access to Vin's business information. *But why?* I wonder. *What is he planning?*

"Think long and hard before you make a final decision," Caleb warns me.

But I already know that I would never turn on Vin and hand private company information or financials over to his rival. The last thing I'd ever want to do is possibly help destroy his business and hurt his family. He's been betrayed before and I'll have no part of it happening again.

Vin protected me and now I'm going to protect him.

"I don't have any access to his computer or files," I lie. I don't know if he's going to believe me or not because the truth is I have all of Vin's passwords. I'm his executive assistant and I'm privy to every last detail. We work together and he trusts me. And that's exactly why I refuse to tell Caleb anything. Not one single word. I won't break that trust.

"Again, think about it very carefully before making a final decision on where your loyalties lie, my lovely. Because if you give me the wrong answer, there will be consequences. I'm a very powerful man, Hannah, but my patience with you is extremely thin right now. Don't try me."

Swallowing hard, I focus my attention out the window next to me and wonder where we're headed. And how exactly I'm going to escape.

18

VIN

After the meeting with the Five Families, I just want to go back to my apartment, shut myself in and nurse my hangover. Of course, I also want to have a pity party for myself. The thought of numbing my wounds with more alcohol briefly crosses my mind, but I'm still too hungover to even consider drinking any more alcohol right now.

My brothers, however, have a different plan. After Carlotta takes off, saying she's meeting Alessia and they have things to do, Miceli, Enzo and Angelo drag me out to a nearby cafe and make me rehydrate with a sports drink and a plate of greasy bacon and some hash browns. It actually tastes damn good and I devour it. After eating, my stomach feels much better.

"So, what's your plan?" Enzo asks me.

"What do you mean?" I finish off the electrolyte water.

"He means are you going to get your shit together and go talk to Hannah or are you going to avoid the situation like a pussy?" Miceli clarifies.

Miceli makes it sound so easy, but facing my feelings for Hannah is anything but simple.

"It's not complicated," Angelo adds, as though reading my mind. "If you like her, make her your girl."

I roll my eyes because Ang has no idea what it's like to fall for a woman. To want her so badly that you physically ache when she isn't near. To think about her constantly when you're awake and dream about her when you're asleep. To yearn to touch her and hold her and give her everything her heart desires.

Yeah, my little brother, the player extraordinaire, has no clue. I can't wait for the day he meets his match. I predict he will not handle it well and I'm going to be highly amused and offer him his stupid advice right back—"It's not complicated. If you like her, make her your girl."

"I think it's more than like at this point, Ang," Enzo says then turns his full attention on me. "C'mon, Vin, If you can't man-up and admit your true feelings—that you love this woman and want her in your life— then you're going to lose her."

"It's so damn easy for you guys to give me advice, but you have no idea how hard this is for me." Dammit, I hate being vulnerable and that's the exact position I'm finding myself in.

"Because of Cynda?" Miceli asks, hitting the nail on the head. Again, he's too damn perceptive because as close as I am to my brothers, I never told them the dirty details of what exactly happened with her. Only that she cheated and I caught her.

Letting out a pent-up breath, I force a nod.

"Did you even love her?" Enzo asks.

I think over his question, a little surprised by it, but not exactly sure how to answer. "We were engaged."

"That's not what I asked."

It's at that exact moment, an epiphany hits me hard and out of the blue. When I compare how I feel about Hannah to how I felt when I was with Cynda...well, there is no comparison. It's completely different. Like comparing rotten apples to juicy oranges.

"I know I never shared the full story of what happened," I say slowly, "but, at the time, all I wanted to do was forget about her. The short of it is I walked into her fucking Allan Meridian up against the wall in the coat closet at a charity gala, and she didn't show an ounce of regret. Instead, she had the audacity to look me right in the eyes then smile right before she came."

Sympathetic curses fill the air.

"I thought she broke my heart, but now with hindsight, I know it was my trust. Because after what you just asked me, Enzo, I don't think I ever loved Cynda. At least not like I love Hannah."

There. I'd said it. I'd admitted my true feelings and it was a relief. It felt like a dam just broke and, instead of water, love began filling my heart. My brothers lit up like the Fourth of July and whooped it up.

"I knew it!" Enzo announces and slaps me on the back.

"I'm happy for you, bro," Miceli says, grinning widely.

"Yeah, same," Angelo adds. "Don't forget who your favorite brother is when you're choosing your best man."

"Me!" Enzo calls out and we all laugh.

"I'm glad you finally got your head out of your ass," Miceli states.

I'm breathing easier now that I've finally admitted my feelings. "Yeah, me, too."

"You better go get your girl before some other man swoops in and woos her away," Angelo says, grinning from ear to ear, his smile bright white and charming. "Like me!"

"Don't even think about it," I warn him. "I just hope she can forgive me for being such an idiot."

"She will," Enzo assures me, and I hope he's right. Otherwise, I really will end up with a broken heart. And I don't think I'll be able to recover this time around.

"Okay, I'm going over to see her and do some serious begging."

"Good luck!" Miceli says.

I'll take all the luck I can get. "Thanks," I say wryly. "Let's hope she's on the same page."

"She looks at you with stars in her eyes, Vin," Enzo tells me and my heart constricts. "She's definitely on the same page."

"Yeah, she's just been patiently waiting for you to realize it and get your shit together," Miceli adds.

I nod, toss them a salute, then hurry out of the cafe. As I head back to my car, I realize that I've been fighting a losing battle this entire time. Every time Hannah managed to punch through one of my walls, I did my best to reinforce it, but she still found weak spots and a way to sneak through. She found the way into my heart and I know I'll never be the same.

Slipping into my car, I start the engine and say the words out loud, "I love you, Hannah." It feels so good to speak the words, to give them life, and I can't wait to tell her. The moment I say them, something happens. It's like the rest of the walls around my heart come tumbling down.

It's time to stop being so miserable and dwelling on the past. Yeah, Cynda was a bitch, but I gave her too much credit. She didn't wreck me for other women; she brutalized my trust and left me fragile and vulnerable. Too broken for any other possible relationship. But Hannah—along with a little help from my brothers and Lottie—has shown me I'm capable of loving and being loved in return. I'm worthy of all the beautiful and miraculous gifts that come with love, too.

I'm finally ready to take a chance. A leap of faith. I just hope and pray that Hannah is, too.

I know I screwed up and I'm going to do my best to prove to her how much I love her and deserve her. Of course, at this point, she might not want me any longer.

No, I don't believe that. Hannah Everson is my woman, my perfect match, and I'd be willing to bet anything that she already knows this and, like Miceli said, she's been waiting for me to figure my shit out and get my head out of my ass.

Prepared to go down on my knees and beg, grovel and plead—whatever it takes—I drive over to Brooklyn and park in front of her building. The first thing I'm going to do is have her move in with me and get her out of this crummy neighborhood. I hate that she lives in a rundown, unsafe area. Not for much longer, though, I assure myself. Very soon, she's going to be sleeping in my bed every single night. I can't wait to wake up to her beautiful face and even more lovely heart every single morning.

Belatedly, I realize I should've brought her flowers or something. I suppose I could walk down to the corner store and see if they sell bouquets, but then quickly decide against it. All I want is to get to her as quickly as possible and make things right again. Then, I promise to make sure my *Angioletto* has fresh flowers every day for the rest of her life.

Her life with me.

19

HANNAH

I have no idea where we're going, but I stay alert, looking for any opportunity to bolt. Caleb drives us to an office building near the docks and parks in the subterranean garage. He walks around the car, opens my door and, the moment I step out, he takes a firm hold of my arm. As he guides me over to the elevator, I can't help but notice how quiet it is and more deserted than I expected. I guess since it's the weekend, nobody is here working. *Great. Just freaking great.*

Once again, I'm on my own. But, it's a place I'm accustomed to being and I have no intention of giving up. Not now, not ever. I'm a fighter and I will go down swinging. As nice as it was being rescued, I know this time around, I'll be rescuing myself. Because as much as I'd like to see Vin appear, I know he has no idea where I am.

A girl can dream, though, right?

No, I immediately scold myself. A girl has to be able to take care of herself and kick some ass when necessary. And that's exactly what I plan to do.

We take the elevator up to the twenty-fifth floor and I'm hoping we run into someone else. But my hopes fall flat as we step out of the elevator into a dimly-lit office. The place is a virtual ghosttown, not a soul around. Caleb finally releases his tight grip on my arm, but where am I going to go? I feel trapped. Deciding to bide my time a little bit and see what he's up to, I force myself to be patient because there's literally nowhere for me to run.

At least, not yet.

"This is my building," he states proudly and all I can think is whoop-de-doo. I mean, seriously, what does he want? A standing ovation?

Congratulations on all your money and being able to buy a building, you piece of shit. As tempted as I am to say it, I press my lips together and keep quiet. He also tried to buy me, too. More specifically my virginity. *Hmmm.* Maybe if he knew that was long gone, he'd lose interest in me. I file that little tidbit to use later.

"And this is my corner office."

La-di-da. What a braggart. It's so unappealing and my gaze skates over the room. It looks like any other office I've ever seen. Nothing special and not nearly as nice as the Rossi Vineyard office. I mean, yeah, the furniture looks expensive and I'm sure it cost a fortune. And, there is a nice view, I realize, wandering over to the big glass window and peering out over the city. But it would take a lot more than this to make up for the horrible man who works here.

"Come here," he says, motioning to me with his hand. "I want you to see something."

Not overly interested, I walk over to where he stands behind his desk, opening his laptop.

"Sit." When I hesitate, he places a hand on my shoulder and pushes me down into the large leather chair.

I hate how he's always manhandling me and realize I much prefer Vin's gentle touch. Gritting back a nasty comment, I wait as he opens a file.

"Look."

I see a bunch of numbers and names of corporations, maybe? Businesses? It doesn't really make any sense to me and I shrug a shoulder, not sure what he's bragging about now.

"I've been slowly buying up stock for Rossi Vineyard. But, it's a secret, so shhh. Don't tell anyone." He sends me a creepy smile and wink.

My attention moves back to the screen and I squint, taking a closer look. *Oh, no.* How much stock does he own? This can't be good. It doesn't make sense that they would sell so much to him. Unless...

"I'm buying it under different corporations I own that no one else knows about. They have no idea that I now own a huge controlling share."

The only reason he would do this is to hurt the Rossi family and their company. But I'm not sure exactly how it all works. Hell, until Vin hired me, I worked at a diner and my biggest problem was sore feet at the end of the day. Not billion dollar corporations and potential sneaky takeovers.

"Why are you doing this?" I ask, wanting to hear his plans so I can run straight to the Rossi family and fill them in on every single detail.

"Control. Majority shareholders have the benefit of voting and election privileges. I'll have a say in the direction the company decides to take. They'll be forced to constantly update me about how the company is performing. And, if I'm unhappy, I can request an election for new board members."

"But why do you even care?" My brow furrows.

"Why shouldn't I?" he asks, voice raising angrily. "They have everything and I'm tired of it. I'm going to usurp some of that power and use it to make even more money. If they want to negotiate, there's only one thing I'll accept."

My stomach sinks. "What?" I ask, dreading the answer.

"I want a seat with the Five Families. And if they don't allow me to join then I'll destroy Rossi Vineyard. I belong on that council, running this city just like the others. I deserve the respect people give them. I want it all," he hisses in a low voice near my ear.

A shiver runs through me and he's even more power hungry and manipulative than I'd originally thought.

"But, why don't we start with you giving me some of Vin's passwords first?"

"I already told you I don't know them. I just answer his phone and get him coffee." I hope I sound convincing enough, but he's looking at me like he doesn't believe a word coming out of my mouth.

"Hannah dear, let me make this clear for you. I'm on the precipice of ruling this city and I'm going to need a beautiful, young wife at my side. The moment I saw you at that auction, I knew it had to be you."

My mouth drops, not expecting to hear him say any of this. That's why he's been pursuing me so hard? He wants a trophy wife? Sorry, but that's not happening. I'd rather die.

"I'm assuming Vin fucked you, claimed your virginity, and it pisses me off that he stole you from me. But I'll get over it. Sure, he may have broken you in first, but I plan to show you so much more. Show you how to embrace pain and turn it into the greatest pleasure you've ever known. So even though he stole your innocence, I know he hasn't introduced you to the dark side. But, I will."

The dark side? I try not to cringe away from him, but I can't help it. I don't want anything to do with that kind of twisted desire or with Caleb. He's a monster and making me want to run, but I need a better plan than that.

"Vin may have bruised my ego when he outbid me," Caleb continues, "but that only gives me more incentive to destroy him. I'm going to take away every last ounce of power from the Rossi's and teach them a lesson. They aren't as great as they fucking think and I can't wait to knock them down a few pegs. And you're going to help me."

Like hell I am.

"And, the first thing you need to do is forget Vin and pledge yourself to me from this point forward."

Even though I should play along with this madman, I can't and, without thinking, I blurt out, "I love him."

Caleb's eyes narrow and, before I realize what's happening, he backhands me across the face. My head snaps and tears sting my eyes. *Oh, God, that hurt.* Beside me, he clears his throat.

"Sorry about that, but don't say ridiculous things like that anymore. Do you understand me?" I nod my head, not daring to look at him, and I see stars at the edge of my vision. "Now, let's go somewhere and have a little chat."

Confused, I frown. Why can't we just stay here? I'm instantly alarmed, but not wanting to get smacked again, I slowly stand up and follow him out of the office. We walk up a flight of stairs and he tugs me through the emergency entrance and onto the roof.

A horrible fear suddenly fills me and I stop walking, my feet digging in and refusing to budge. But Caleb is stronger and yanks me forward, right over to the edge.

"It's a spectacular view from up here, isn't it?" His fingers are digging into my upper arm and he leans over to look out at the city, pulling me with him, right up to the edge.

My heart and stomach sink. We're so high up, twenty-six floors to be exact, and falling would mean certain death. I glance around, wondering how I can escape. It's much louder up here than I would've expected with lots of vents and machinery. Chewing on my lower lip, I'm grateful for some potential places to hide, if I need to.

"I wouldn't recommend falling, though. It wouldn't end well." He smirks at me. "So, here's the situation, Hannah, and I'm going to be brutally honest with you. And before you blurt out something stupid about love again, I suggest you think hard first. Okay?"

"Okay," I force out when his hand tightens around my arm harder, like a damn vise.

"I'm going to rule this city, with or without you by my side, but I'd like you to be my queen. However, you need to forget about Vin Rossi, stop working for him, and help me humiliate him in every possible way I see fit." I squirm, trying to loosen his grip, but it's proving to be impossible. "Starting with those passwords. If you don't agree to give them to me then I'm sorry to say I have no use for you."

As if he needs to reinforce his threat, he suddenly releases my arm and grabs the back of my neck, forcing me against the low brick wall and pushing, making me look out over the edge and down at the sidewalk below. My hands grab hold of the edge, holding tightly, and my heart is thumping madly. Caleb makes sure I have a good view down to the sidewalk and it's dizzying and terrifying all at once.

At that moment, staring twenty-six floors straight down to the unforgiving pavement, I realize that if I don't agree to his mad plan then he's going to kill me.

With a cry, I twist, drop and manage to break away from him. Scrambling to my feet, I'm halfway to the door when his arms wrap around me and he hauls me roughly back against his chest. Disgust fills me when I feel his erection pressing into me. My fear is turning him on and I squeeze my eyes shut. He's enjoying this and I want to vomit.

"You feel that?" he whispers in my ear. "I'm going to put my cock into every hole in your body and you're going to enjoy it. I might even make a new hole with my knife and then fuck that, too. Because, you owe me your innocent blood. But you gave it to Vin," he practically snarls.

His words make me sick.

"That's right," I hiss and slam an elbow backwards, right into his side. He grunts, loosening his hold slightly, and I take advantage and make a quick escape. Unfortunately, he's so much faster than me and he grabs me again.

I let out a scream as he drags me right back over to the edge again. "That wasn't very smart, Hannah. All you've managed to do is make me angrier."

Then, Caleb roughly yanks me up off the ground, his fingers digging cruelly into my hips. He shoves me forward, until the front half of my body is dangling over the side of the building and I'm staring straight down to the ground.

Terrified, I don't dare move or even breathe. I'm at his mercy and if he lets go, I'm dead.

"This is the last time I'm going to ask you, Hannah, you little bitch," he growls. "Will you give me the passwords to access the documents I want?"

With no other choice, I yell up to him, "Yes! Pull me back up, please, and I'll do whatever you want."

The asshole lets me hang there, precariously suspended above the city for what feels like another minute before finally pulling me back up. Relief floods me and I sag forward, terror thrumming through my veins.

"See how easy that was?" he asks, grinning at me.

I don't think my heart will ever slow down and I hate Caleb Durant with a passion. I have no intention of giving him what he wants or betraying Vin and his family, but I needed to buy more time. I just hope the plan forming in my head works or I have no doubt that Caleb will toss me off this roof without a second warning.

20

VIN

When I reach Hannah's apartment, I'm nervous as hell and hesitate before knocking. It was easy to get inside because the damn lock on the front door is broken and I make a mental note to have that taken care of for her. Even though I plan on moving her out of this dump as soon as possible.

Here goes nothing, I think, and lift my fist. Heart in my throat, I knock and wait, listening closely, expecting to hear her move around inside. But the only thing I hear is silence. Maybe she's in the bathroom. I try again, louder this time. After waiting a few moments, still nothing, so I pull out my phone and send her a text. No response. What the hell? I call, too. It rings and rings then drops into her voicemail.

"Hannah?" I begin pounding, hard and loud enough that she will definitely hear. Pressing my ear against the flimsy door, I strain to hear something, but it's far too quiet. Maybe she went out. I know she likes to walk down to the cemetery and visit her mother's grave. But why wouldn't she message me back?

"What's all the racket about?" a cackly-old voice grumbles.

Turning around, I see one of Hannah's neighbors peering out of her doorway. If I remember correctly, her name is Liza.

"I'm here to see Hannah," I say, stepping away from the door. "I guess she's not home."

"No, she's not. I saw Hannah leave earlier, but..." Her voice trails off and I frown, not liking the strange look of concern that passes over her wrinkled face.

"But what?" I ask warily, walking closer. "Did something happen?"

The woman hesitates and I try to make her feel more comfortable.

"I'm Hannah's boyfriend, Vincentius, and you're Liza, right? Hannah's mentioned you to me."

"That's right. I've seen you around here."

I nod, encouraging her to keep talking.

"Hannah is a good girl. She hasn't smiled much since her mom died. But she smiles with you."

My heart clenches within my chest.

"She was with a man and I didn't like the looks of him." She crosses her arms firmly beneath an ample chest. "No, siree, not one little bit."

"Why not?" I ask, suddenly feeling ill as the old lady began to describe a man who could only be Caleb Durant.

"And then it looked like she didn't want to get into his fancy red car, but he forced her, anyway. I almost called the cops, but then didn't. My son says I need to let people live their lives and stop getting into their business."

"In this case, it's okay, Liza," I assure her, "because the man who took Hannah is a very bad guy and I need to know exactly what you saw so I can find her."

179

"There's not much else to tell. I was watching from inside, so I couldn't see too much. But, I do remember him grabbing her, far too roughly, and they seemed to have a bit of a scuffle on the sidewalk."

The idea of Caleb manhandling my woman makes my blood boil. I'm going to find that asshole and bury him for touching her. With a sharp nod, I thank Liza and hurry down the stairs and outside. My gaze sweeps the area, looking around and imagining how the situation with Caleb and Hannah played out. And my fury increases.

On a whim, I try calling her phone again. From somewhere close by, her phone's ringtone fills the air. It's slightly muffled, but close, and I spin around, listening closely, trying to figure out where it's coming from. My gaze dips and I spot the edge of her phone sticking out from beneath the bushes. Leaning over, I swipe it up and examine the screen's cracked surface. I also see all of my missed texts and calls. *Dammit.*

A horrible sense of dread washes over me and panic has me yanking my phone out and calling Miceli.

"Hey, Vin," Miceli answers. "How'd it go with—"

"She's gone!" I interrupt, unable to mask the alarm in my voice.

"What?"

"Caleb took Hannah and I don't know where they went and I'm freaking the fuck out."

"Okay, calm down," Miceli says in an even voice. "We'll figure this out and find her."

"I have a really bad feeling," I continue, the pit in my stomach growing. "She needs me, Miceli. I think she's in trouble and I have to find her!"

"We will," he states firmly. "I'm going to have my men start looking, but I need all the details you can provide that might help."

"I talked to her neighbor—it sounds like Durant abducted her right outside her apartment building. He has a red BMW, the sporty kind that costs way too much money."

"I'm going to have Leo start checking CCTV footage, see if we can pick up their trail. And I'll have my men start scouring the city."

"Okay. I'm going to drive by where the bastard lives."

"Keep me posted, Vin, and keep it together. We're going to get your woman back."

After hanging up with my brother, I jump into my car and realize I don't even know where Durant lives. "Fuck!" I slam my fist against the steering wheel. Forcing myself to calm down, take a deep breath and think logically, I consider what I do know. And I know where his office building is—it's a big, ugly brown building downtown near the docks.

Something deep in my gut tells me to go there. I have no idea why and I don't question it. My gut is always right and has never let me down before. Right before I caught Cynda cheating on me, I remember having little niggling feelings of doubt. At the time it didn't make sense; but, with hindsight, it makes perfect sense.

Hitting the gas, I turn my car toward Caleb's office building. It's probably locked up tight because it's the weekend, but wouldn't that be a perfect place to take Hannah? It's quiet, empty and who knows what he might do?

But why would they go there? Fuck if I know, but that's what my intuition is whispering. So that's where I go.

21

HANNAH

My heart is still thumping wildly after the incident on the rooftop and now we're back in Caleb's office. He shoves me down into his chair again and I'm staring at his computer screen as he pulls up the homepage for Rossi Vineyard.

"Log in," he demands.

If I log in under my own name and password, there's no important information that will come up. But, we will be connected with the network and, from there, I'll need to enter a different password to get into Vin's side of things.

"C'mon," he urges me, hovering over my shoulder, giving me a little shove.

Very slowly, I log in and watch as I'm granted access to the network.

"Okay, now log into Vin's restricted access portal."

Trying not to let my hands shake, I type a fake password, knowing that after three attempts, I'll be locked out of the entire system.

Incorrect. Try again.

Beside me, Caleb frowns. "What did you type in? You better not have fucked up on purpose," he threatens me.

"I'm sorry!" I cry. "But you're making me nervous."

Once again, I type in some random letters and numbers and hit enter.

Incorrect Password. You have one more Login Attempt.

Caleb's hand grabs the back of my neck and squeezes so hard that I yelp. His fingers dig into my flesh and he snarls, "Stop playing games."

"Maybe he changed it," I suggest weakly.

"For your sake, I hope not."

This is it. My last chance and then we'll be completely frozen out. And that's exactly what I want. I refuse to give Caleb access to Vin's private files and intel that will help him destroy Rossi Vineyard. *No fucking way.*

Knowing I'm about to unleash the beast, my fingers hover over the keyboard a moment before I quickly type the wrong password and hit enter.

Access Denied.

"You bitch!" Caleb roars and shoves me forward roughly.

If I didn't have such quick reflexes, my forehead would have smashed into the computer screen. But I manage to dart to the side and then drop right out of the chair, quickly moving out of Caleb's reach.

He isn't far behind, though, and it's scary how fast he can move. My head stings as he grabs a handful of my hair and yanks me right off my feet. With a cry, I fly backwards and drop down to the floor. He rips my head back, fingers still tangled viciously in my hair, and hisses, "Big mistake, Hannah. Now you're going to suffer the consequences."

Even though I'm in an awkward position, I manage to remember a move I learned a long time ago in a self-defense class. *Go for weak and vulnerable areas.* And, right now, the only weak area I can reach is his face. Launching my hand around, I poke him right in the eyes, hard and with zero hesitation. Caleb screams and instantly releases me.

Falling backwards, I quickly spin around onto my knees, crawl out of his reach and clamber back up onto my feet. *Nice try, asshole.* Determined to get out of here, I race out into the hallway, avoiding the elevators, and go for the stairwell instead. I don't have time to wait around for a slow elevator and I know Caleb is going to be hot on my heels in just a moment.

Once I shove through the stairwell door, I head down, racing forward like a bat out of hell. I'll run all the way down to the lobby and escape through a door on the first level. Even if the main entrance is locked, there has to be an emergency exit or security patrolling around or something!

Feet pounding down the stairs, I make it down three floors before I hear an ominous click. *What the hell is that?* I wonder. Pausing, breathing hard, I listen for the sound of heavy footfalls coming from above, following me down, but it's quiet. Eerily silent. Then a voice sounds over the loudspeaker and a chill slashes down my spine.

"The building is in lockdown. You won't be able to open any door, Hannah. There's no way out if you're heading down. But good luck... because here I come..."

There's a click as he signs off and sheer terror has me spinning around and doing the only thing I can—running back up the steps. Once I reach the next landing, I try to open the door to the twenty-third floor, but Caleb wasn't lying. It's locked and won't budge.

"Oh, shit," I whisper. Trapped, not sure what to do, I know I need to go up. Heading down is a death sentence. Maybe if I can make it back onto the twenty-fifth floor, I can somehow avoid Caleb and hide. Unless that door is locked, too, like he said.

With no other option but up, I run fast, my legs burning and lungs heaving. Just like he warned, the door to the twenty-fifth floor is also locked. What the hell? Cursing, I force my feet to continue up and come face to face with the door to the roof. My hand shakes hard as I reach out, warily push the bar, and it swings open. Even though I know this is a bad idea, what else can I do? With zero options, I step outside and the wind hits me hard causing my hair to whip wildly around my face.

My awareness is at an all-time high as I take a few, tentative steps out onto the rooftop. Other than the helicopter landing pad, there's a lot going on...places where Caleb can be hiding just out of sight. My gaze scans quickly over all the loud mechanical and electrical systems, including the stuff for heating, ventilation and air conditioning units. I didn't get a good look earlier, but I take a moment to study things more closely now as I search for an escape. Or, a hiding spot. Along with the sounds of traffic coming from below, it's super noisy so I don't hear Caleb move up behind me until my peripheral vision catches sight of him.

Before he can grab me, I bolt forward, weaving between equipment, doing my best to elude him. But, realistically, how much longer can this cat and mouse game go on? There are only so many places to hide up here and once again panic rears its ugly head.

If he catches you, you're going to die, I tell myself. It's as simple and horrifying as that. *Now move your ass because no one is coming to your rescue this time.*

My inner cheerleader can be quite blunt, but also extremely motivating. Running around the HVAC system, I duck down by some kind of vent and wait. I think my heart dropped out of my ass while running away from Caleb. Fear can do that to a girl.

"Oh, Hannah...Come out, come out wherever you are," Caleb calls in a sing-song voice.

Biting my lip, I stay frozen in place, but also ready to bolt.

"You can run, but you can't hide," he continues taunting me.

Tears threaten, but I hold them back, forcing myself to be ready for anything. I can't let this asshole win. I refuse. There has to be something I can do. Some way to get the upper hand. Glancing around, I search for some sort of weapon. My desperate gaze falls on a toolbox, barely visible, and sticking out from around the corner. Hope springs up inside of me. If I can get my hands on a hammer or something then maybe I can hit him on the head and knock him out.

Dropping down low, I crawl forward on my hands and knees, getting closer and closer to the partially-concealed toolbox. I reach it without incident and quickly scan the contents inside. *There's my hammer.* Grabbing the hammer in one hand and arming myself with a screwdriver in the other, I stand up and peer around the corner.

Where is he?

In answer, Caleb steps out from behind a ventilation system and my hopes crash and burn. He's holding a gun and it's pointed directly at me. A smile curves his mouth.

"Nice try," he says, motioning to my measly excuse for weapons. "But, Hannah, my dear, you just brought a knife to a gunfight. Or, should I say a hammer?" He laughs at his own stupid joke and I realize how incredibly screwed I am.

One-hundred percent fucked. Right up the ass.

Keeping as much distance between us as possible, I start slowly side-stepping, and we begin circling each other. It really is turning out to be some kind of gruesome showdown and I wave my weapons out in front of me.

"Stay away from me," I hiss, doing my best to appear threatening.

"You can't win, Hannah, so stop playing games."

"You think I'm going to just give up without a fight? No way."

"You're just going to make this harder on yourself," he tells me, moving closer. "Maybe you haven't noticed, but there's only one way off this rooftop. And that's down."

My nostrils flare and the wind seems to be blowing harder than ever. Swiping my hair back and out of my eyes, I wish I had taken the time to pull it back. *Oh, well. Too late now. Focus, Hannah. Take this jerk down.*

Instead of answering, I put on my toughest face and swing the hammer when he moves closer. Clearly, it doesn't have the desired effect I'd like because he chuckles.

"Did you ever see that movie? *The Shining*? Remember when he's stalking up the steps after his wife, getting closer and closer, and she's swinging that hammer at him? Threatening her husband? Trying to hurt the man who loves her?"

"You don't love me!" I shout above the racket of machinery. "All you want to do is hurt Vin and I won't let that happen!" Cranking my arm back, I throw the screwdriver as hard as I can, watching it cartwheel through the air, and praying that it stabs him in the chest. Instead, he easily sidesteps it and my heart sinks.

No, no, no.

"You're really making me angry, Hannah," he snarls, spittle flying out of his mouth. "This could've been so much easier. So simple. But, no! You have to be a bitch about everything, don't you? A first-class cunt who I'm going to take great pleasure in ending."

"Leave me alone!" I cry then spin around and run. He shoots the gun and a bullet hits the HVAC system and I yelp in surprise. Luckily, his aim isn't great and I keep moving, not daring to stop and look over my shoulder. A few more POP, POP, POPs fill the air, but he keeps missing, thank God, and then he lets out a howl of rage that curdles the blood in my veins.

I stumble out from behind some equipment and, suddenly, there's nowhere else to hide. Finding myself in dangerously open territory, facing the helipad, I run forward, zigzagging to avoid any more shots, and find myself far too close to the edge of the building for comfort.

Now what? I wonder desperately. I don't have the luxury of time to stand around and make a logical decision, so I just run and pray. The truth is I am trapped up here and, sooner or later, he's going to catch me.

Unfortunately, it's sooner than I'd like.

Once I cross the helipad, I feel Caleb ram into me and I cry out and lose my balance. Stumbling forward, I hit the ground hard and scrape my palms and knees all up. Somehow, I manage to hold onto the hammer, though. My knuckles are white, my grip like glue, and I know it's my last shot to do some damage. Ignoring the stinging scrapes, I'm shoving up to my feet when Caleb grabs my hair again and hauls me forward. Crying out, my feet drag along the pavement, and I twist my body, trying to swing the hammer and make contact with his side. I'm fighting him hard, but to no avail. He's so much stronger and his absolute fury just gives him more strength.

Caleb pushes me against the edge and my gut slams into it with an *oomph*, knocking all the breath from my lungs. Then he grabs my wrist, holding it out over empty air and shakes it so hard that I release the hammer with a yelp, scared he just broke bones.

As the hammer plummets to the ground below, I hope no one is walking by on the sidewalk. It's going to do some serious damage when it lands.

"You had your chance, Hannah, but you fucked up. And, if I can't have you then no one will."

Suddenly, he grabs me and lifts me right up off my feet. My hands claw onto him, refusing to let go, and I manage to dig my fingers into his forearms and hook an ankle around his leg. As I tilt backwards, holding on for dear life and looking up at the sky, a scream tears from my mouth.

My last thought is of Vin and how much I regret not telling him that I love him.

22

VIN

Stalking back and forth outside of Durant's office building, I wonder if my gut was wrong? I've circled the building three times and all the doors are locked. There are no security guards roaming around either because I keep looking, wanting to flag one down and let me inside. The whole situation is beyond strange.

Frustrated, I rake a hand through my disheveled hair and wonder what to do next. I hate that I feel so out of control. Are we out of leads already? Just as I'm debating whether or not to leave, my phone rings.

"Tell me something good," I say in answer and quickly realize I'm on a three-way call with Miceli and Enzo.

"The neighbor was right," Miceli states. "CCTV footage caught Caleb forcing Hannah into his car and taking her to his office."

"I saw the whole thing," Enzo adds. "Where are you?"

"I'm at the office, but—" I step back and look up, trying to see some sign of life. "It's locked up and dark. I can't get inside."

"They're there," Enzo states, voice firm. "You need to get inside. Hang on, bro. I got an idea."

Enzo goes silent and I wonder what he's cooking up. While my older brother is very perceptive, my younger brother is extremely resourceful.

I'm still looking up when, all of a sudden, I see something falling through the sky. *What the hell is that?* I wonder. Squinting, I jump back out of the way and the next second a hammer lands on the sidewalk, cracking th pavement where it hit into a million little pieces and shooting chunks of concrete up. Several pieces hit my leg and I frown at the sting.

"Holy fuck!" I exclaim. Moving back, I try to get a better view of the roof when I hear a scream pierce the air. My heart sinks, but instant relief fills me. Hannah is alive and she's close. "She's here. On the roof."

"Get to her, Vin," Miceli growls.

I make a frustrated sound and hurry over to the main entrance again. "Maybe I could break the glass, but if he has the elevators on lock-down…if she's trapped up there…*fuck.* I'll never make it in time."

Enzo jumps back on the line. "Angelo is up in his helo and now he's on his way to you, Vin. He's going to fly you up to the roof. There's a helipad up there. Be ready."

Oh, thank Christ. "ETA?" I ask, my nerves in knots.

"Three minutes."

Hang in there, Hannah. I'm coming.

Heart in my throat, I pray that's enough time. *Just outsmart him a little longer, baby. Please. I can't lose you. Not when I need to pull you into my arms and tell you how damn much I love you.*

Waiting for Angelo and worrying about Hannah makes the next three minutes the longest ones of my life. I'm about to lose my damn mind when I finally see the helicopter approaching. It wouldn't draw any special attention because lots of helos fly all around the city at all hours of the day and night. If you can afford it, it's a much easier and faster way to travel and sure beats sitting in traffic.

Angelo expertly lands in the middle of the damn street and, luckily, we're not in the middle of the main streets in the busy downtown district. It's much quieter by the docks, especially right now when no one is working. Otherwise, I would've had to play traffic cop and that might've gotten dangerous. A few cars drive past, eyes wide, as I run toward the helicopter and jump inside. I'm barely in and it's already lifting, the rotors loudly *whomp-whomp-whomping*. My brother gives me a salute and up we go.

Fuck, I hate heights. But, for Hannah, I'd do anything. Even if it means facing my biggest fear.

I don't bother to close the door and I hang on tightly, watching as the ground gets further and further away. *Hang in there, Angioletto. I'm coming.* As we up, passing office windows, Angelo slips me a Glock 19 which I tuck in the back of my waistband. Hopefully, I won't need it, but it's better to be prepared than sorry.

I think Angelo missed his calling as a military pilot. He's amazingly skilled and calm behind the controls. One moment we're heading up and the next, Ang is lowering the helo down on the large H on top of the building.

I instantly spot my woman. She's bent over the edge of the building, hanging on for dear life, and fighting off that bastard Caleb Durant. Without waiting for the helicopter's skids to touch, I suck in a deep breath then leap out of the open door and land in a squat. Popping up, I race forward, hellbent on saving Hannah from that asshole.

The noise of the helicopter landing has already alerted Caleb to our presence—it's not like there was any quiet or sneaky way we could've pulled off a helo rescue—and he pulls Hannah back onto the rooftop and spins, eyeing me with such hatred it's palpable.

"Let her go!" I yell above the rumble of machinery and the helo's rotors. Hannah slumps in relief, but we're not out of this yet. My gaze locks onto hers and I telepathically tell her to drop, to get out of the way. At the same time she falls down, I yank the gun out and point it at Caleb. "It's over, Durant! Give it up!"

I spot his gun on the ground which he must've dropped earlier and kick it away, making sure it stays far out of his grasp. *Time to end this.*

I motion for Hannah and, the moment she starts crawling towards me, Caleb grabs her again, yanking her up in front of him and using her as a goddamn shield. Fury fills me and I hesitate, watching in horror as he takes a step back. Everything in me goes numb as he lifts Hannah off her feet and it's clear he has every intention of tossing her over the side.

No fucking way.

"Don't move!" I yell, warning him, but he's lost it. Instead of heeding my warning, Caleb turns, lifting Hannah higher, and I don't have a clear shot. I won't risk hitting Hannah. I also won't stand here and watch Caleb toss her to her death.

Thinking fast, I race forward, lower my pistol and shoot at his leg. POP! With a scream, Caleb drops and Hannah twists away, finally breaking free. She turns and runs to me, and I catch her in my left arm, my right one still holding the weapon on Caleb. It's hard to tell what damage I caused, but I don't think it's much more than a graze. Just enough to slow him down.

"Get in the helicopter," I say, pressing a quick kiss to her temple. "Go!"

Hannah does exactly as I ask. *Good girl.* Turning my full attention back to Caleb, thankful that Hannah is now going to be safe with Angelo, I stalk forward, ready to deal with this bastard once and for all.

Even though my gun is still trained on him, Caleb Durant is unhinged and desperate. Without warning, he launches himself at me and we go flying backwards. I hit the ground with a thud and the gun goes flying out of my grip. Caleb and I roll around, throwing punches, practically recreating the scene at the restaurant. But, instead of moving further away from the building's edge, we roll right up to it.

The asshole is furious and hopeless which makes him more dangerous than ever before. Stronger, too. We scramble up and he grabs hold of my shirt and shoves my back against the ledge. My balance wobbles and I feel my entire body tilting backwards, right over the side. The sky flashes above and I grab onto him tightly, panicking. *Fuck, I hate heights.*

I can't let go or I'll be the one falling to my death.

Then everything happens so fast it's a blur. I hear Hannah scream my name, followed by the pounding of feet. A gun fires and, right before Caleb can shove me over the side, his eyes go wide in shock. Blood leaks from the corner of his mouth and his eyes roll back in his head. His body begins to fall forward and that's not good. Right before he can slam into me and send us both tumbling out into nothingness, I shove my hands against his chest, pushing him to the side and rolling in the opposite direction. I drop out of the way in the nick of time as Caleb goes tumbling forward, arms windmilling, and his scream of denial pierces the air making my skin crawl. And then he's gone.

"Vin!"

I spin around and stagger into Hannah's open arms. For a long moment, we hold onto each other, the wind whipping hard around us. A sense of relief floods through me. We're safe. It's over.

"Are you okay?" I ask, pulling back and looking her over. "Did he hurt you?"

"I'm fine. What about you?"

"I'm okay, if you're okay, *Angioletto*." I press a kiss to her lips, savoring her taste and warmth. So damn grateful that we're both alive. I'm never letting this woman go. Not ever again.

Behind us, Angelo clears his throat. "Time to go, lovebirds. The police are going to show up soon and I don't want to be here when they do."

I turn to my brother. "Thank you, Angelo. For everything."

"Any time, bro. But let's hustle."

"Miceli will take care of everything," I assure him.

"As he always does. And, thank God for that. I'm far too young and too good-looking to be rotting away in some jail cell."

Hannah's arms are wrapped around my waist and a hint of a smile plays at her lips. Together, we walk back to the helicopter.

"Everything that happened up here was self-defense," I say and he nods.

"Durant lost his damn mind," Angelo says.

"He wanted power," Hannah tells us. "He talked about joining the Five Families and destroying the Rossi family."

I snort then help Hannah up into the helo. "Never would've happened." Once we're situated, we put our headphones on and Hannah continues to tell us what happened between her and Durant. Even though he's dead and will never be a problem again, anger fills me. If I could kill him all over again, I would. And, this time, I'd be the one to put the bullet in him.

"He wanted access to your files," Hannah continues. "He said he was going to take control of Rossi Vineyard, that he was buying up stock under various companies, and then he was going to destroy the entire thing."

I exchange a look with Angelo and make a mental note to discuss the entire situation with Miceli later. My brother will handle it and the rest of us will help with whatever he needs.

"I refused to give Caleb the password," she says.

My heart kicks up a notch. Her loyalty is astounding. "Even though he threatened you?" She nods and I frown. "But why? You should've just done it."

But my girl shakes her head vehemently. "No. I'd never let him hurt you or your family. *Never.*"

"Oh, Angel…" I pull her closer, tucking her against my side. As much as I fought this—fought my feelings for her—there's no denying the truth. I am head over ass in love with Hannah Everson and I can't wait to tell her just as soon as we get home.

23

HANNAH

Once we're safely back on the ground, Vin and his brothers go into damage control fast. I give them a full recounting of what happened and how Caleb bought up a bunch of stock and planned to destroy them from the inside out. After telling them everything I know, Vin takes me back to his place, and he tells me to eat something and try to relax.

I hate watching him walk away when all I want is to stay locked in his embrace, but he and his brothers have things to do. "Can I help you?" I ask as he's leaving again.

"You can help me most by staying here where it's safe. We have an emergency meeting with the Five Families and some serious damage control to do. I don't want to worry about you on top of everything else, okay?"

I nod and he kisses me. Before it can become too intense, Vin pulls back. "I'll be back as soon as possible. Promise."

The big apartment is so quiet without him and I hope everything is going to be okay. I'm not sure how it will be when Caleb Durant's broken body is lying on the sidewalk outside of his building. But, then again, we're talking about the five most powerful mafia families in the city. Disposing of a body probably isn't anything new for them.

While Vin sets things right, I realize how hungry I actually am. I can't even remember when I ate last because so much has been going on. Vin's fridge is stocked full of fresh ingredients and I love the fact that he's a good cook. He's also very modest about it, but that man can whip up a plate full of deliciousness with ease.

After searching through some tupperware, I sit at the island and eat some pasta salad with fresh basil and mozzarella. My thoughts keep returning to Caleb Durant and how things could have ended so tragically. If Angelo hadn't already been out flying, he never would've made it to Vin in time to reach me. But he came flying in at the last minute and flew Vin up to save the day…and then Angelo ended up shooting Caleb and saving Vin before he went over the edge…

My stomach and heart is still all twisted up and thinking about what could've happened is wrecking me. I quickly lose my appetite, clean up and decide maybe a shower will help relax my nerves. Because they're completely shot.

I walk into Vin's large bathroom and turn the shower on, adjusting the water until it's the perfect temperature. As I strip out of my clothes, I catch sight of myself in the mirror and pause. I see bruises I didn't even know were there, thanks to the awful way Caleb had roughly dragged me around. I'm also scraped up and, now that every-thing is quiet, things are starting to ache and sting.

Hopefully, the warm water will help soothe my frayed nerves and bruised body. I step beneath the spray, grateful that I'm still alive. And, of course, that Vin is, too. The fact that things could've ended so very differently and so much worse will always haunt me.

After washing my hair, I pour some of his shower gel on a washcloth and lather up. *Mmm.* It smells just like him—a citrusy, slightly spicy fragrance that has me yearning for him. As if in answer, Vin suddenly appears and I freeze when I spot him through the steamy glass. He quickly sheds his clothes, opens the shower door and steps inside.

His electric green gaze slides down my naked body like a caress and then he pulls me into his arms, kissing me passionately. Like it's the last night of the world and we're the only two left. Wrapping my arms up around his neck, I lean into his warm, wet, very aroused body and kiss him back with every ounce of love in my heart.

I haven't told him yet that I love him and I don't think I can wait much longer. But his hand drops between my thighs and he starts doing deliciously wicked things. Dropping my head back, gasping as his fingers slide into my wet core, I whimper and moan and writhe. Vin knows just how to touch me and I'm climaxing fast.

"More…" I beg, kissing down his wet chest. "I need more, Vin. I need all of you."

When I wrap my hand around his huge, pulsing cock, he groans. Then he scoops me up, turns and presses my back against the cool tiles.

"If that's what you want, then that's what you'll get," he says, pushing the head of his cock between my folds. With one powerful thrust, he fills me and I tighten my legs around his waist, hanging on for dear life as he begins to power into me.

"Oh, God," I gasp. He's stretching me like never before, filling me up, and nothing has ever felt so good. So very right. At this moment, I give everything to Vin—my mind, my body and my heart. It's all his.

"Come for me, *Angioletto*," he rasps, increasing his pace and massaging my clit until I'm biting down on his shoulder to stifle my screams. "That's it. Let me hear you scream my name as you come on my cock."

"Vin!" I cry as my inner muscles squeeze tightly, milking his cock. The orgasm pummels me and he groans, shuddering hard as he erupts inside me. The water falls over us and our rapid breathing fills the steamy air. We stay connected like that for a long, precious minute, his cock buried deeply, our breaths hard and fast and intermingling.

Then he sweeps my wet hair back and whispers raggedly, "I love you."

My heart speeds up and I tighten my arms around him. "I love you, too. So very much."

After another squeeze, Vin slowly pulls out and sets me back down on my feet. "You can't even begin to understand how much," he says, cupping my face in his large hands and staring intently into my eyes. "If anything would've happened to you today—"

"It didn't," I assure him, placing my hands over his. So much passes between us at that moment. All the love we have for each other and all our hopes for the future.

"Thank God," he whispers, dropping his forward against mine.

Vin and I rinse off quickly because the water is getting cool. He shuts it off, grabs a big, fluffy towel and wraps me up in it. Before I can move, he sweeps me up into his arms and carries me to his bed, gently laying me down. Crawling in beside me, Vin turns on his side to face me. He studies me so intensely and I know he wants to say something, but he hesitates.

"Tell me," I whisper, running a hand through his disheveled hair. "Whatever you're struggling to say, you can tell me, Vincentius."

It's the first time I've ever used his full name and he reaches out, takes my hand and squeezes.

"I fought this—us—and I'm so ashamed that I did. You're the best thing that ever happened to me, Hannah, and I am so damn sorry for pulling away and hurting you. I was just...scared."

"Scared of what? I would never hurt you."

"I know that now. My past kept holding me back."

"Your ex?"

He nods. "We were engaged and I was young and naive. I thought I loved her."

"What was her name?"

"Cynda Drake. Why?" He arches a brow.

"Because I need to know her name so I can add her to my dead-to-me list."

"It's that like your shit list?" he teases, mouth edging up.

"It's worse."

Vin chuckles and places a kiss on the back of my hand. "She cheated on me. Most likely multiple times, but I walked in on her with an acquaintance and the sight of them fucking left permanent damage. It's like everything inside me froze and I walled off my heart and swore I'd never let a woman get that close again. Promised myself that I'd never get emotionally involved or let down my guard. And it worked…until I met you."

"You mean the day you saved me at the auction and spent a fortune?"

"I'd spend anything to save you. Don't you know? You're priceless, *Angioletto*."

"Thank you, Vin," I say softly. "If Caleb had won me—"

"I refused to let that happen."

"Why?" I ask, genuinely curious about what made him spend so much money on a stranger.

"Because when I looked at you up there, I saw a woman hurting, vulnerable and scared. I vowed to get you out of there and I didn't care how much money it took or who I needed to outbid."

"Vin…" My heart expands so much, it hurts.

"I also saw an angel who desperately needed help."

"More like a damsel in distress."

"No, an angel. You're good and kind and pure, Hannah. There was no way I was going to let a cretin like Durant defile you."

My throat tightens with emotion and I can't speak for a long moment. So, instead, I kiss Vin with all the love I'm feeling in my heart. "My hero," I whisper. "I can never repay you for all the times you've come to my rescue."

"I don't want you to repay me, Hannah. All I ask is that you love me."

"I'll love you forever and ever and ever," I promise, crawling up and straddling his powerful thighs. "And I'm going to seal that promise with a kiss."

Settling back, I take his cock and begin stroking until it's rigid again. Then I lean down and lick the tip before wrapping my lips around his firm length and sucking him deep.

"Ahh, Jesus, Hannah," he moans, hips bucking up off the mattress.

I lick and suck, holding him tightly, squeezing gently, and paying close attention to what he likes and responds to. And it seems that he likes everything I do. Before he comes, Vin pulls me up and slides me forward.

"Get on my cock, Angel."

I'm a little surprised he didn't finish in my mouth, but I do as he says. Very slowly, I line up his throbbing cock with my entrance and then sink down, taking him to the hilt. We both groan and I begin to move my hips. Leaning forward, finding the exact right angle, I rub my clit against his pelvis and take the lead.

As we soar together, finding our bliss, for the first time in a very long time, I feel like I'm not alone anymore. Vin is my new home and I know that he will always love and protect me.

24

VIN

I can't believe how stubborn I'd been about admitting my true feelings for Hannah. Waking up with her in my arms after telling each other over and over all night how much we love each other is the best feeling in the world. It's like I'm walking on sunshine or a rainbow. With Hannah in my arms, it's like I'm holding a piece of heaven.

And I'm never letting this amazing feeling or woman go.

I'm not sure how long I lay there and watch her sleep before her lashes flutter open. She gives me a shy smile and I lean in and kiss her.

"Oh, no," she murmurs, pulling back. "I need to brush my teeth and—"

"You don't need to do anything except kiss the man you love," I say firmly then capture her mouth in a long, slow, very thorough exploration. She moans into my mouth, sliding her fingers through my hair and I'm instantly hard.

I'd love to lounge around in bed with her all day, but I have plans. Plans that can't wait another minute. Pulling back, I grin at her. "Do you trust me?" I ask, searching her bright blue gaze.

"Of course," she instantly responds.

"And you love me?"

"More than anything." Her brow furrows and she sits up. "Why are you asking me these questions? Should I be nervous?"

"No. But I'm going to need you to get dressed and come with me. Before I forget my plans and make love to you instead."

She gives me a lazy, very sensual smile and reaches for my lengthening cock. "Would that be so bad?"

I force myself to roll out of bed and ignore the aching need that has my dick pointing straight up to the ceiling. "Plans," I say again, trying to ignore the lust thrumming through my body.

Hannah chuckles and slides out of bed. "Okay, okay. These plans of yours better be good."

I pull her against me, wrap my arms around her and kiss her once more. "They involve making you my wife," I whisper. "If you'll have me?"

Dropping down onto one knee, I take her hand in mine and look up into her startled blue eyes.

"Will you marry me, Angel?" I ask. "Because I can't live without you."

Hannah's mouth drops open and tears brighten her already vibrant eyes. "Yes," she whispers. Then her brow furrows comically. "Are you sure?"

I burst out laughing. "I've never been so sure of anything in my life." I pull her down and we kiss and kiss and kiss. And maybe we get a little bit of a later start than I'd originally planned, but it was worth it. So damn worth it.

After an impromptu romp—this time on my bedroom floor—we get dressed and I whisk Hannah to the courthouse. I can't wait another minute to make her officially mine. I promise her we can do it all over again if she wants a big wedding, party, white dress and the whole nine yards. But, she sweetly reassures me that all she wants or needs is me. Only me.

Standing before the judge, I hold Hannah's hands and we face each other. For a man who swore never to get emotionally involved with a woman again, I've sure come a long way. All thanks to an angel who saved me just as much as I saved her.

The ceremony is short and sweet. Once we are declared man and wife, everything in my world feels right for the first time since I can remember. Hell, maybe ever. Hannah is officially mine. My wife, my partner, my love, my best friend and my future.

I kiss her and she pushes up onto her toes to seal the deal.

"We did it," she whispers, smiling up at me with stars in her eyes.

"I love you, Mrs. Rossi," I tell her. If she has stars in her eyes then mine must be glowing with twin suns.

"I love you, too, Mr. Rossi."

Once we're out of the courtroom, Hannah squeezes my hand. We haven't let go since we walked in the door. "Should we call your family?"

"Yeah, I'd like that."

I call Miceli and tell him our good news. He congratulates us, not sounding surprised in the least, and Alessia is there, too, because I hear her squeal of delight. They tell us to come over immediately because they're going to throw us a big, celebratory feast. Even though I want to take my bride straight home and back to bed, I know she wants to celebrate. I suppose I can wait a little longer. Even though I'd much rather be skin to skin with Hannah.

"Stop!" She giggles.

"What?"

"That look you're giving me!"

"What look?"

"Like you want to rip my clothes off."

"I do," I growl, sliding my hand over her ass and squeezing.

"Behave, Vincentius," she reprimands me and tosses me a playful look.

"With you? Never." I pull her up, tighten my arms around her and kiss her hard.

After we leave the courthouse, I drive us straight over to Miceli and Alessia's. They live in a gorgeous penthouse, high above the city, and I think my anxiety over heights has gotten a little better. After nearly falling off that rooftop, being in here doesn't feel too bad.

All of my siblings, along with Leo Amato and Gia DeLuca, are already there. They all congratulate us, showering us with hugs and endless good wishes. I notice that Leo and Gia look very cozy together and my nosy sister later confirms they're seeing each other.

"How do you know everyone's business, Lottie?" I ask her teasingly, nudging her arm.

"I can't help it if I'm so trustworthy that everyone wants to confide their secrets to me." She innocently bats her lashes and we all laugh.

For as quickly as Alessia and Miceli threw this party together, it turns out amazingly. They call in a favor from a friend who owns a nearby Italian restaurant and within two hours, the long dining room table is full of fresh, hot entrees. There's also a delicious-looking cake with flowers on top. I'm in awe that they did this for us, much less did it all so fast. My family is truly the best.

I'm on my third glass of champagne, but notice Hannah is only drinking lemonade. "Anything I should know?" I joke.

"Just that champagne bubbles upset my stomach," she tells me, snuggling closer.

The idea of Hannah having my baby thrills me to no end. Seeing her belly round and swollen with our child doesn't scare me at all. In fact, it has quite the opposite effect. If I have my way, it won't be long before we start our own family. I don't want Hannah to ever feel alone again and I plan to give her as many children as her heart desires.

After eating far too much food, someone turns the music up and we're all dancing and having a good time. Hannah and I share a slow dance and then the music speeds up. I watch as she dances and laughs with Alessia, Lottie and Gia. My angel has never glowed more brightly.

My brothers linger nearby and talk, and little Nico bounces around in his swing. Enzo nudges me with his elbow. "Never thought I'd see you this happy, bro."

I can't help but smile wider. "Thank you, Enzo. If you hadn't given me your invitation, I never would've gone to that auction and met Hannah."

"Well, I'm glad that kinky auction helped you find the love of your life."

"What about you?" I ask. "Have any potential ladies caught your interest lately?" Now that I'm happily settled, I'd love to see the same happen for Enzo. Even Angelo and Carlotta, but they still have time. I can't help but remember the way Enzo and Gabriella Bianche were looking at each other.

"Me?" He huffs out a sardonic chuckle. "I'm married to my job. You know that."

"Yeah, and I'd sworn off women. Things change."

But, he shakes his head. "No one special on my radar and seriously doubt there ever will be. You know me—love 'em and leave 'em."

"I thought that was more Ang's style."

207

"Yeah, well, it's mine, too. Work comes first then, if there's time, I might play." His phone starts vibrating and he pulls it out of his jacket, glances down at the caller ID and frowns.

"Business?" I ask, knowing full well that it is always business.

His scowl only deepens at my question. "I need to take this."

I hear Angelo bark, "Why are you calling me?" as he stomps away. For a moment, I'm curious as to who it is he's talking to, but then my beautiful wife appears, wrapping her arms around me, and I instantly forget about everything else.

"Hello, Mr. Rossi," she murmurs, her hands sliding up over my shoulders, her fingers locking behind my neck.

I press a kiss to her lips and pull her closer. "Hello, Mrs. Rossi." My hands caress up and down her back, so very tempted to dip and curve around her ass.

"Have I told you how much I love your family?"

"They are pretty amazing. But I think you should meet my parents."

Hannah pulls back, eyes widening. "I'd love to."

"Then how about a honeymoon trip to Sicily?"

"Are you serious?"

"Of course. And I have no doubt that they're going to love you."

"Not as much as I love you," she declares.

My grin widens and I've never been more happy in my life. "Are you ready to blow this joint?"

"Already?"

"I was ready to go an hour ago," I tell her, pulling her tighter against me, letting her feel my arousal.

"Oh, my. Well, in that case, we probably should. I want to make sure my husband is happy and well taken care of."

"You can take care of me all night, Angel. And I will happily return the favor." She giggles and then I kiss her deeply. How did I get so damn lucky?

My wife. My life. My angel.

25

EPILOGUE

HANNAH

A few weeks later, I'm sitting beside Vin on a comfy, cushioned rattan couch on the sunny back porch of his parents' Sicilian villa. Salvatore and Carmela Rossi are in their mid fifties and I can see where Vin and his siblings get their good looks from. The older couple is still striking and so full of life. Their energy and humor are contagious and their enthusiasm and zest for life makes me smile. When Vin and I are their age, I hope we're exactly the same way.

We've been out here, laughing for the past hour, and enjoying getting to know each other better. I'm so glad we came here to visit and I adore his parents. Of course, a part of me wishes Vin and my mom could've met. I've told him how much she would've loved him. He comes with me to the cemetery and we visit whenever I feel the urge to be closer to her. Although I know she's in my heart and always will be, I still like to sit beside her grave and bring her flowers.

And there are always plenty of fresh flowers to bring her because Vin brings me flowers every single day. He loves spoiling me and always puts my happiness and well-being above all else. I'm not sure what I did to deserve him, but I am so damn grateful.

After finishing some delicious limoncello, Carmella tells the men she wants to spend some time alone with her new daughter-in-law. Then she links an arm through mine and leads me forward, past a bubbling fountain and into the fragrant gardens.

"You, my dear, have brought love back to my Vincentius and I can never repay you."

A blush steals across my cheeks. "I love your son very much."

"Oh, I know. I can see it. You both glow with *amore*." She sends me a knowing look. "He wasn't always like this, as I am sure you are well aware. Vincentius had been deeply hurt before."

I nod and let out a soft sigh. "He told me about what happened and how his heart had been broken. It was hard at first—getting him to open up and tear down his walls—but I'm so glad he's finally let me in. I wasn't sure he would."

"Because Vincentius overthinks everything."

I burst out laughing. "He does!"

Carmella's next words, so very wise, make my chest tighten. "Trust the overthinker who says he loves you. Because he's thought of every reason not to."

And I know she's right. Vin fought his feelings for me, but now I have no doubts in his love and that he will always be there for me and with me. Forever.

As the week progresses, I enjoy my time thoroughly, but begin feeling strange. My stomach has been extra queasy and I even threw up the other day which I never do. I've also been getting easily exhausted and needing afternoon naps. Something feels different and I assumed I was getting sick, but by evening I'd feel back to my old self.

After throwing up again the next morning, I'm down on my knees, hugging the toilet bowl, and Vin stands behind me, holding my hair back and massaging my back.

"I think you should go to the doctor," he states, sounding worried.

"My doctor is in New York," I grumble. Sitting back on my heels, I swipe a hand over my face.

"We have doctors in Sicily, Hannah."

Out of nowhere, the nausea passes and when I start to stand up, Vin grabs my elbow and helps me up. "I'm already feeling better," I insist, but Vin shakes his head.

"I'm not taking any chances. Let's just see what the doctor says. Okay? Please. For me."

"Okay" I reluctantly agree, unable to tell him no. Even though I'm not a big fan of going to the doctor's office and being poked and prodded unless it feels like I'm on the verge of dying, I decide to do this more for Vin than myself.

I'm surprised when the doctor shows up at the house later that afternoon. "A house call?" I ask, completely dumbfounded.

"C'mon, Dr. Adami will check you out in our bedroom. He's been our family physician for as long as I can remember."

Trusting Vin, I place my hand in his and meet Dr. Adami. He's very nice and sets me at ease right away. After asking me some questions in heavily-accented English, he asks if he can take some blood. Even though needles aren't my favorite thing, I roll up my sleeve and squeeze my eyes shut, clutching onto Vin's hand as Dr. Adami fills a syringe.

After that's done, he tells us he's going to check my blood and will call us later with the results. Glad that's out of the way, Vin and I end up lingering in the bedroom, getting frisky up against the wall. Then over on the bed and then somehow we end up on the floor. At that point, I've exerted quite a bit of energy and I'm feeling drained again, so Vin pulls me into his arms and we lay down together on the bed.

Curling up against his warm body is relaxing…so very soothing…and I listen to our rapid heartbeats slow down and begin to beat in unison. I'm just drifting off to sleep when Vin's cell phone starts vibrating. He presses a quick kiss to my head and stretches an arm out, grabbing his phone off the nightstand.

"Hello?" he murmurs. I assume it's one of his brothers, but he doesn't say anything for a long moment. The minutes stretch by and I'm dying of curiosity. Then, Vin says, "*Grazie,*" and hangs up.

"Who was that?" I ask.

"Dr. Adami." His voice sounds hoarse and I frown.

Oh, no, is something wrong? He looks so serious and I instantly assume the worst.

"Oh!" I pull back and sit up, eyeing him closely. "What's wrong? What did he say?"

Vin slowly sits up and his green eyes lock hold of mine, looking a little stunned. "Well, he said you're pregnant."

My jaw drops. "Oh, my God." I'm trying to get a read on him and I think he's just as surprised as I am. Granted, we have been having unprotected sex ever since our hot encounter in his car, so it shouldn't be too shocking. Still, the idea that I'm going to be a mother makes me so nervous and excited and, suddenly, I'm sweating because Vin hasn't said a word and I have no idea how he's feeling. "Vin…are you happy?"

"I've never been happier in my life," he says and clears his throat. "There's, um, more."

"More?" My heart sinks. "What do you mean?"

"He mentioned higher, ah, hCG levels than normal."

What does that mean? Panic fills me. "Is something wrong with the baby?"

"No, no he said those kinds of levels usually mean…multiples."

My brow scrunches together, not quite understanding what he's saying. "Multiples?" I echo. "I don't—"

Then it hits me. *Oh. My. God.*

"Twins," he clarifies.

"Holy shit," I exclaim, feeling shell-shocked.

"Yeah, holy shit."

We both burst out laughing and then Vin pulls me into his arms and kisses me hard.

I instantly melt against him like I always do. We kiss for a long, passionate minute and then I pull back, staring into his bright green eyes. "I can't believe it."

"He said you'll need an ultrasound to be sure, but chances are pretty high there's more than one baby in there."

"The idea of one is crazy enough, but *two*?" He still looks a little shaken and I squeeze his hand. "Are you sure you're okay?"

"I think my heart just exploded. I couldn't be more okay."

His words bring me so much joy.

"You're going to be a daddy," I whisper, cupping his face.

"Hannah…" He says my name softly, almost reverently, and leans his forehead against mine. "I've never known happiness like this before. I love you so damn much, *Angioletto*."

Vin lowers his hand and places it over my still-flat stomach.

"I'm going to love this little baby—I mean, babies—fiercely."

"I know you will," I say and press a kiss to his lips. Vin is going to be the most amazing father in the world. I have no doubt in my mind. "Should we go tell your parents?"

"In a little bit," he murmurs and begins kissing the side of my neck. "First, let's have our own little private celebration."

Sounds good to me, I think, and tilt my head, giving Vin better access. His lips are warm and soft and heat instantly floods me. Only Vin can do this to me and I get to spend the rest of my life with him.

I'm not sure what I did to get so lucky.

But, it's official. I love my life.

EXCERPT: HIS TO OWN

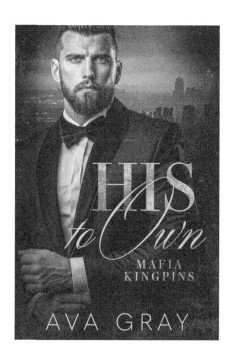

He's supposed to marry her older sister, but he can't stay away...

MICELI

The mafia world is cold and cruel. I live by one rule - cut their throat before they cut yours. It's what keeps me ruthless and on top of my mafia family.

But when I see something I like, I take it. It's no different with Alessia DeLuca, who's supposed to marry my rival... while I'm marrying her older sister.

When Alessia sees something she shouldn't, kidnapping her is the only logical answer...

Taking her cherry sure isn't.

ALESSIA

Ever since I met him in a mix-up, I've been intrigued by Miceli Rossi. He says he always gets what he wants, and it's obvious he's obsessed with one thing only... me.

He can force me to marry him. He can even force me to wear his ring.

But I'll make sure I'm the worst wife he could have.

Anything to make sure he doesn't realize how much I want him.

His to Own is book one of the **Mafia Kingpins series. This is a full-length standalone novel with these tropes: age gap, mafia, V-card, surprise pregnancy. Guaranteed happy ending!**

Alessia

I've never been so nervous in all of my twenty-four years. Pacing across the room again, I know I must be wearing a trail in the carpet, and I finally pause and wring my hands. My older sister Gia—older by two years—doesn't look even a fraction as anxious as me.

A quick glance at the clock reveals it's only a couple of minutes until eleven.

"How can you be so calm?" I ask. "I'm about to pass out or poo my pants. And you look like you're about to take tea on the lido deck."

She snorts back a laugh. "Because, sis, there's no point in getting worked up. Our fate has already been decided." Gia flips her long, dark hair over a shoulder and sends me a perfect smile. And it is flawless. Everything about Gia is—from her slender figure to her high cheekbones to her polished and refined manners. She should've been a model. Or, the queen of some faraway country. I swear, sometimes I wonder if she sweats or burps or ever feels like she's going to poo her pants like me? She's a classic beauty and always appears so in control. Even when she's not.

Me, on the other hand? I'm a hot mess. I worry, I stress and I obsess. That, of course, leads to the sugar cravings that I can't seem to control. Grabbing another piece of candy from the small bowl on my nightstand, I unwrap the watermelon deliciousness and pop it into my mouth, sucking until my cheeks cave.

"But, we're about to meet the men we're going to marry," I say with a frown. "Men we've never met."

Gia sighs in that worldly way of hers. "What do you need to know? They're both extremely handsome and powerful. An alliance between our family and both of theirs will secure the DeLuca name and increase our importance in this city."

Something I care very little about, but I don't say that. My father, Aldo DeLuca, is an important figure in New York City's Italian mafia. Although, he's not quite as powerful as The Rossi or Bianche family. That's why he's planning on marrying me off to Rocco Bianche and Gia to Miceli Rossi.

My stomach turns when I think about the stranger I'm about to go downstairs and meet. A man I'm just supposed to say "hello" to and then "I do" without any time to get to know him.

He's a stranger! I want to scream. This is so old-fashioned and ridiculous. Or, am I the one who's overreacting? Gia is quite content to marry Miceli and she's never laid eyes on the man. But, she's already had a serious boyfriend and been intimate with someone before. Maybe that's why this isn't as big of a deal for her. But, I've never been in love much less had a relationship and sex or explored any of that. God, I feel like such a baby. A naive little girl. Because the truth is it's more than just sex I've been missing out on. The truth is, I've never even been properly kissed by a man. I mean sure, there were a few quick kisses here or there when I was in school over in Italy. But those were boys who I met in town and saw a movie with. Now, I'm dealing with an experienced man who's going to have expectations and desires. How in the world am I ever going to please him?

Biting my lip, my frown deepens.

"Stop scowling like that," Gia comments. "Or you're going to make your wrinkles look deeper."

My head snaps up. "I have wrinkles?" I march over to the mirror and examine my face with a critical eye. Well, of course, I have frown lines between my brows. Doesn't everyone?

"Yes, Lessi, and the way you're always worrying, you're going to look like an old lady in a few years if you keep it up." She stands and stretches. "That's why I don't let anything bother me and use so many face creams."

Smoothing my index finger over the lines, I try to flatten them. I certainly don't want to look older than my years. Maybe I'm going to need to snag one of my sister's many potions or lotions. She's in the know about all the latest when it comes to looking younger and having gorgeous skin.

"Well, I suppose it's time to meet my fiancé," she says without a trace of emotion.

My heart rate kicks up and I start wringing my hands again.

Gia walks over and squeezes my arm. "You look like you're about to puke, Lessi. Relax. Why are you so worried, anyway? Just go downstairs and talk to the good-looking man for a little bit. Be agreeable, smile and laugh at his jokes. Easy, right?"

Easy for her maybe, but not for me. "Yeah, okay," I mumble. Watching Gia whirl away without a care in the world makes me green with envy. I wish I could be more like my sister. But we're pretty much opposites in every way. While she's tall and slender, I'm short and curvy. She's calm and easygoing, I'm anxious and high strung. And, she's a social butterfly. The boys at school all loved and chased her everywhere while I preferred to stay in my dorm and spend a quiet evening reading or studying.

Maybe I'm just wound too tight and being with Rocco Bianche will help loosen me up and learn to enjoy life more. But, for whatever reason, something about him doesn't feel right. Clasping a hand over my stomach, I wonder if I'm going to be sick. *Stop being so dramatic*, I scold myself. *Get it together and go down and meet your fiancé.*

Grabbing another piece of candy, I unwrap it and pop it into my mouth. I don't know why sucking on sweets calms me down—at least a little—but I pause and grab a handful of the candy, tucking them into my pocket. Better to be safe than sorry. Because I have a feeling I'm going to need every single one of them when I go face my husband-to-be...a complete and total stranger, as of this very moment.

Walking out of the safety and comfort of my bedroom, I head to the back staircase which will take me down to the library where Rocco is waiting. As I walk down the steps, I wonder if I should've dressed up more or put more makeup on? Gia looks like she just stepped off a runway and I look...well, like I always do. I didn't put any extra effort into my appearance and I wonder if that's because a part of me doesn't want Rocco to find me attractive? Because I want him to tell my father he isn't interested in marrying me.

Hmm. A devious, little plan begins to form in my brain. Maybe I should purposely try to turn him off. Do something unlady-like or be quiet and mousy, refusing to make polite conversation. Or...maybe I could tell him I'm in love with someone else. Make up a boyfriend and pretend I can't get married because I love someone else.

No, that won't work. He would probably just get annoyed and then go ask my father who would quickly deny the existence of my fictional man.

Standing right outside the library now, I hesitate, needing a moment to get myself together. Pushing my nerves down, I force myself to unclasp my hands and let them hang at my sides. Then, I pull in a deep, steadying breath and walk through the doorway.

A very tall man stands in front of the windows, his back to me. A very broad back with wide, muscular shoulders visible through his suit jacket that tense the moment he hears my soft footsteps on the carpet. The first thing I notice is the sharp cut of his lightly-stubbled jawline as turns and when he's fully facing me, my heart thumps harder. Holy hell, the man is insanely good-looking. I didn't expect to be face to face with a Greek adonis and I suck in a sharp breath.

With a naturally tanned complexion and thick, dark brown, slightly wavy hair slicked back off his gorgeous face, he makes me grab onto a nearby chair for support. Eyes darker than the deepest espresso focus on me and, maybe I'm imagining it, but I think I see approval. And maybe a wave of relief, too.

The other thing I immediately notice about him is he exudes power. And it has nothing to do with his perfectly-tailored black suit. It's the way he carries himself and the purposeful way he walks toward me. His vibe screams "I'm in charge" and you better listen to every word that comes out of my mouth.

Which, by the way, is a beautiful mouth. His lips look soft, very kissable, and the dark stubble gives him a dangerous look. It also makes me want to reach out and lay a hand against his cheek so I can feel its rough texture. The boys I've known were exactly that—boys with clean-shaven faces. This is a man in every sense of the word and when he extends a large hand, I glance down at it, suddenly at a loss and forgetting basic manners. I'm too fascinated by the groove that appears on his left cheek when he gives me a small smile. A freaking dimple that makes my stomach flip because it's the only thing about him that looks slightly boyish.

"It's nice to meet you," he says, voice so deep I can feel it rumble through my chest and roll all the way down, down, down to my toes.

"You, too," I force out as his huge hand encompasses mine like a soft-ball mitt. Our gazes lock and I stare into eyes that are so dark brown they're almost black. Our hands hold for a moment too long and his intense gaze makes me uneasy. Uneasy and utterly mesmerized.

When he finally releases my hand, I let out a shaky breath.

"Shall we sit?"

I nod and follow him over to the couch. Keeping my distance, I carefully sit down a couple of feet away and instantly clasp my hands in my lap.

"You're not what I expected," he murmurs, his voice low and almost to himself.

I can feel him studying me and I shift under his thoroughly penetrating gaze. "Oh? And what did you expect?" I ask, daring to look over and up.

He leans closer, eyes narrowing slightly. "Not you."

When he doesn't elaborate, I can't help but burst out laughing. Maybe it's my nerves making me be inappropriate or maybe I'm starting to feel a tiny bit more comfortable in his powerful presence. Which is the oddest thing. How can I be feeling less anxiety when I should be feeling more? But something about him is almost...I don't know. Familiar? It makes no sense.

"What's so funny?" he asks, his eyes searching mine.

"I have to admit, I didn't expect this at all, either."

His mouth edges up and my attention zeroes in on that dimple. "Really?"

I nod, unable to stop smiling. Maybe this situation isn't as bad as I originally thought it would be. Marrying a stranger still scares the bejesus out of me, but if he's a calm, kind, gorgeous man who can put me at ease and take his time, be patient with me, then perhaps I'd be willing to try.

"I know this whole situation is awkward," he says, as though reading my mind. "And our families are being...pushy. But I want you to know, I'd never force a woman into marriage. If you're truly not interested in getting to know me better, I'll walk away."

"You would?" Of course, I lean forward and this makes me like him a little bit more.

"Before you make a final decision, you should know a few things first," he says, eyes bright and a little mischievous. "Some women consider me quite the catch."

"Oh, I'm sure," I say teasingly and chuckle. *Oh, my God, I'm flirting with him. And he's sitting here trying to sell himself.* A man like him doesn't need to convince a woman to be with him, but here he is being all adorable and a little unsure. And, I like that. Confidence is nice, but arrogance is a huge turn off to me. I'm glad that he's wondering and maybe not quite as self-assured as normal.

"That's right. They like the fact that I'm wealthy, powerful and, modesty aside, fairly attractive. That is, if you like the cliche." The way he says it makes me grin. Almost like he's making fun of himself.

"Cliche?"

"Tall, dark and handsome." He sends me a devastating smile.

Oh, I do! I scream internally. More so than I ever even realized. But, I play it cool and send him a smirk. "Oh, I don't know. Normally, I prefer short, fair and homely." He knows I'm joking and his eyes crinkle in the corners in the most adorable way.

"Really?" He huffs out a laugh.

I shrug a shoulder. "But, perhaps, I could be persuaded to expand my horizons."

He slides closer and my heart threatens to burst from my chest when his powerful thigh brushes mine. I'm holding my breath as he reaches for my hand, lifts it to his lips and brushes a kiss along my knuckles. "Then I'll do my best," he says in a low voice.

Swallowing hard, I bite down on my lower lip and a zap of awareness shoots through my body. The brief touch of his lips has me squeezing my thighs together and I can't seem to look away from his eyes. They're like a deep, dark swirling black hole, sucking me in deeper with every passing second.

The attraction between us is palpable and I smile. He's still holding my hand when he says, "So, Gia, tell me about yourself."

Gia? What is he talking about? *Oh, God.* My heart sinks as it belatedly occurs to my befuddled brain that I'm sitting here swooning over Miceli Rossi.

My sister's fiancé.

Oh, for God's sake. Then where the hell is the man I'm supposed to be marrying? And how am I ever expected to want him after meeting this amazing man?

"Um, I think there's been a mixup," I murmur, and his dark eyes narrow.

Read the full story HERE!

SUBSCRIBE TO MY MAILING LIST

I hope you enjoyed reading this book.

In case you would like to receive information on my latest releases, price promotions, and any special giveaways, then I would recommend you to subscribe to my mailing list.

You can do so now by using the subscription link below.

SUBSCRIBE TO AVA GRAY's MAILING LIST!